THE THREE LEGGED MASTER

LOHIT J M

To Shiva,

Who is everything, yet exists as nothing.

Contents

Preface

To be frank, I had to Google what a preface is and what it typically contains. Here's what I found: "A preface is an introductory passage written about a book by its author. It lays out why the book exists, its subject matter, and its goals."

Sincerely, I have no illusion that I would become rich and famous after publishing the book. Nor am I writing it to fulfill any purpose of mine. Nor do I expect the reader to be transformed after reading the book. Then, why am I writing this?

When the seed sprouts, it's a relief to Mother earth. When the cloud bursts, it's a relief to the weight of the sky. When the pain is expressed, it's a relief to the deeply held emotion.
When the stories come out, it's a relief to my life!

Acknowledgements

- To my parents, without whom I wouldn't have existed.
- To my wife Amulya, who stood by my side and helped me with editing and proofreading. For all the aesthetics of this book belongs to her.
- To Sadhguru, for helping me to get closer to clarity and see things just the way they are.
- To Kartik & Haarika who selflessly proofread the novel and suggested changes which led to the refining of the story.
- To Rahul and Aishwarya, for designing a beautiful cover page and helping in proofreading.
- To Akshay Nadiger, who helped me in the publishing process of the novel.
- To my school friends and college friends, without whom the story would not have formed.

CHAPTER I

Arrival Of Master

As I unlocked the gate of my house after my morning jog, I felt as if I had just run a marathon. I only jog sporadically, usually when I notice my stomach protruding, which reminds me that while I am still a seventeen-year-old in the outside world, I seem to be an aging man in the belly department. Although I dream of having six-pack abs, for now, my "dad bod" will have to suffice. Jogging is not a regular habit for me; it's more like an occasional occurrence, similar to Christian festivals. I only do it to impress girls, as there is a misconception that having a great body compensates for having a small brain. However, truth be told, my brain is just average, like most things in my life. I'm still figuring out my true identity. My friends call me with all sorts of names that I can't freely express and my mom affectionately calls me a "lazy bum." My name is Rahul, as seen on my marks card.

Born in 1990, a time when the world hadn't yet drowned in technology and wasn't adrift in intoxications. Those were the days when children still heeded their parents' melodious scoldings, when neighbors felt like family, and Sunday evenings were reserved for watching movies together. With just Rs. 2 in pocket money, you could fill half your stomach. Capturing a photo with a 32-reel camera was a highly anticipated moment, filled with meticulous planning and the excitement of seeing those upright faces without any hint of melodrama. Those days, letters still held the warmth of handwritten emotions, carrying tales of well-being and cherished connections across distances.

Cassettes, with their crackling melodies, were like treasures unlocking a trove of memories, transporting us back to the sweet simplicity of old songs and the emotions they evoked.

As I approached the door of my house, I heard a faint whimpering coming from the neighbourhood. The man who lives there is like a real-life version of Count Dracula, with his gloomy, gothic mansion that sends shivers down my spine. He's always alone, and I can hardly recall seeing him smile or leave his ominous abode. Meanwhile, my friends boast about the pretty girls who live in their neighborhoods, and I am here with a creepy old man. It's as if they're living in a rom-com, and I'm stuck in a horror movie! Initially, I paid little attention to the yelping, but as the sound grew louder, my curiosity got the better of me. Eventually, I saw the source of the noise: a German Shepherd puppy with only three legs. This was the first time that I was seeing anything like that in the bungalow man's house. As I watched the little guy hobbling around on his remaining limbs, I couldn't help but feel a bittersweet mix of sorrow and compassion for the poor little guy.

My mother emerged to see what I was up to, and she transformed into that of a typical Indian TV serial aunty. I had seen this side of my mom many times, and the melodrama was unbearable. "I feel so sorry for that cute little dog. Maybe I should feed it something," she exclaimed.

"Mom, it's sad that a three-legged dog can elicit sympathy from you, but not your two-legged son. I'm starving. Feed me first," I retorted.

"Okay! Let's go inside," she conceded, and I followed her like a hungry puppy.

• • •

The next morning, sun crept into the room and I had no intention of waking up early for my jog. It had become a habit of mine to give up on things and the jog was just another item on the long list. So, instead, I found myself lazily lounging on the couch, eyes glued to the TV screen, watching the latest astrology predictions.

It always puzzled me why people spent so much time trying to peek into their past or future, instead of living in the present moment. But then again, this wasn't my own thought - it was a statement made by my teacher, whose words usually went in one ear and out the other. He would always lecture us about living in the present, but he did so by watching a channel called 'Sanskar'. Meanwhile, we preferred MTV and V - channels that catered to our youthful tastes.

As I watched the TV, my mind wandered to the newly found dog that I had stumbled upon yesterday. Curiosity getting the better of me, I made my way outside to the compound wall and peered through a tiny hole. And there it was, curled up in a corner, playing with a piece of leather. Its peaceful demeanor reminded me of a dear friend who had also lost a leg. Despite her struggles, she never lost her spirit. I could still hear her words echoing in my mind: "Never say that I have lost a leg, and always say that I have one leg." She lived a life of poverty and hardship, but her smile and determination never faltered. Looking back, I realized that my time with her was some of the best moments of my life. It hurts to think that she was gone, but the memories of her strength and spirit lived on.

I couldn't help but feel a twinge of sorrow as I thought of my dear friend. She was the body that nobody wanted, but her soul was what everyone craved for. Her passing still felt like an open wound, raw and tender, and I missed her dearly.

In stark contrast, the many girls that I had chased after had all eventually drifted away, leaving behind only the faint echoes of memories. None of those memories could compare to the time I had spent with my friend. As I looked at the dog, a sense of longing and melancholy washed over me, reminding me of the void that my friend had left behind. I felt a strong urge to spend more time with the dog, to bask in its warmth and to feel the comfort of its presence - just like I had spent with my dear friend.

• • •

I yearned to take the dog out for a stroll, hoping it would evoke memories of my dear friend. I vaulted over the compound wall, untied the dog's chain, and led it out. The dog didn't bark, but instead wagged his tail, as if we were already friends. My plan was to take it out for a walk, play for a bit, and sneak it back before the old man noticed.

As we walked down the road, the dog happily limped around. I tugged it onto the footpath from the road, fearing an oncoming vehicle might hit it. Although the pavement was uneven, I felt it was safer than the road. However, the dog didn't seem to agree and headed towards the road.

We passed by vast mansions, and I dreamt to be in one someday. Suddenly, I noticed a blind lady struggling to cross the road. I decided to assist her, and took her hand to lead her across the street. I left her on the sidewalk, but she declined to walk on it, asking me to leave her by the road. I was taken aback and explained to her how dangerous it was to walk on the street, but she replied, "My son, I cannot tell the difference between the rough pavement and the street since I am blind. The road would be easier for me." Her words struck me profoundly, and I obeyed her wish, hoping she would be safe.

I looked at the dog and I saw how helpless it was in expressing its difficulties, just like the blind woman. It made me ponder how often we assume what's best for others without considering their own wishes and struggles. Feeling a renewed affection for the dog, I kissed his head. "Let's go home, Master," I said, realizing that he was the real master, teaching me a valuable lesson that no textbook could ever teach.

• • •

It was the first day of our 11th standard. Our school offered both 11th and 12th grades. All of my friends — Kiran, Arvind, Nizam, David, and Gopesh — had decided to go to school together on that day.

Amongst our group of friends, we had distinct characters that added color and diversity to our gang. Kiran, affectionately known as Fatso due to his insatiable appetite, was a jovial and plump member of our group. Arvind, the tall and well-built lad, had an appearance that caught the attention of every girl, yet we boys knew him for his occasional lack of wit. Nizam, the mischievous one in our gang, found joy in teasing and playfully taunting each member. David, the silent and dependable person, always came to the rescue whenever any of us found ourselves in trouble. Lastly, Gopesh, the studious member, shouldered the responsibility of ensuring that every member of our group successfully passed their exams.

"How do you feel about going to class after such a long time?" I asked, curious to hear my friends' perspectives.

Arvind, with a nostalgic tone, expressed, "I still miss my village. Those were the days when we roamed freely through the fields, relishing mangoes, swimming in the stream, and visiting the vibrant evening bazaars. There was no pressure to achieve anything; it was the most carefree and relaxed time of my life."

Just as we were absorbing Arvind's sentiment, David, who came from a wealthy background, interjected, "During the break, my family and I went on a trip to Europe." His interruption brought a momentary shift in the conversation, highlighting the contrast in our travel experiences.

Kiran added, "And we went to the US." His remark, surpassing David's trip, added another layer of wealth-driven experiences to the discussion. The rest of us exchanged glances, acknowledging our limited travels, mostly confined within our state and often centered around temple visits. A mix of jealousy and excitement stirred within us.

But Nizam, breaking the pattern, proudly exclaimed, "I had been to UK!"

Everybody burst out laughing and we knew that Nizam would not have gone anywhere beyond from his native place.

"UK means Uttara Karnataka" he said trying to make everyone laugh. But nobody laughed at it because he makes that joke every time he comes back from his hometown.

As we finally arrived at the school, our lively conversation dissipating, we were met with a disconcerting sight. Our PT teacher stood near the gate; his stern gaze fixed on the students who had arrived late. It was clear that he was reprimanding them for their tardiness.

Gopesh, gripped with fear, expressed his concern, "Bro, this PT teacher is definitely going to give us a hard time. We're already 30 minutes late."

Attempting to reassure us, David chimed in, "Don't worry, we'll try to win him over with some flattery. It's our first day, so maybe he'll be a little lenient if we plead our case."

As we approached the school gate, our PT teacher stood there, ready to greet us with his trademark bitter speeches delivered in a peculiar butler-like English accent. He held a whistle, its shrill sound notorious among the students. However, it was not the whistle itself that struck fear into our hearts; it was the long thread attached to it.

The sight of that thread sent shivers down our spines, for we knew all too well what it meant. The thread was a symbolic representation of the dreaded punishment that awaited any student who dared to cross the line. It was a tool of discipline, a means for our PT teacher to keep us in line, instilling a sense of fear and respect.

"Why late today?" the PT teacher shouted, his voice filled with impatience and authority.

Quickly thinking on his feet, Nizam lied, "Bus late, Sir." It was the most common excuse used by students, hoping to escape the consequences of their tardiness.

Unsatisfied with Nizam's response, the PT teacher probed further, asking, "Bus late means why you late?"

Nizam, caught off guard, replied with a hint of sarcasm, "Because I was in the bus, Sir."

Suppressing our laughter, we tried our best to keep straight faces. Nizam continued to stare at the teacher.

The PT teacher's stern voice broke through the momentary distraction, reprimanding us, "Don't act smart. What are you seeing me? Is monkey dancing on my head"

Internally, we couldn't help but silently agree, murmuring to ourselves, "Monkey is not dancing, it is talking to us." However, we wisely kept those thoughts to ourselves, not daring to utter them aloud.

Apologizing quickly, we responded in unison, "Sorry, Sir."

Continuing his interrogation, the PT teacher turned his attention to Nizam's footwear, questioning, "So, why wearing chappals to legs today?"

Nizam quickly responded, "I have a small wound on my leg, Sir."

Unsatisfied with the answer, the PT teacher demanded, "Show me your leg finger."

Navigating the delicate situation, Nizam reluctantly showed his toe, hoping to convince the teacher of his valid reason for wearing chappals.

It was a moment filled with tension and a touch of amusement, as we awaited the PT teacher's verdict.

Nizam, though tempted to show his middle finger in his mind, wisely kept his thoughts to himself. Instead, he complied with the PT teacher's request, showing his finger that appeared to be in good condition, aside from a minor scratch.

In response, the PT teacher erupted in anger, shouting, "Don't lie with me! I don't like"

For a moment, everyone exchanged glances, sharing a sense of embarrassment, while our PT teacher remained blissfully unaware of his unintended remark. The fortunate circumstance in this situation was that we were all boys, providing a small measure of relief.

Feeling a mix of fear, laughter and frustration, Nizam quickly apologized once again, uttering a meek, "Sorry, Sir. Can I leave for the class" However, deep down, we all knew that our apologies held little genuine remorse.

The PT teacher's anger reverberated through the air, creating a tense atmosphere. He abruptly ordered Nizam, "understand and stand with me!"

Our PT teacher had murdered both English and us at the same time. But we had acted as if everything was normal and it was our mistake and it was his right to punish us.

It was David's turn next.

"Why wearing no belt today" asked the PT teacher. We were astonished at how he could observe every little part of us, when we hardly noticed it.

"My mom took it for washing," replied David.

"You also go wash" replied the PT teacher with anger. His English was suffocating and at the same time entertaining.

"I will wear tomorrow Sir" requested David.

"What you wear tomorrow? What about today? "came the counter question.

"Sorry Sir", came the reply. This was the only dialogue which would convince and console a heartless, English-less teacher

"Round the ground and stand with Nizam". Replied the teacher, indicating David to run around the ground with confidence that even an English professor would lack.

Likewise, he reprimanded all of us and made us stand under the tree.

"Now, everybody stand in the straight circle and sit up 10 times" said the teacher. We forgot geometry lessons for a moment and wondered what a straight circle is. But we were used to the scolding and the actual meaning behind them.

As we stood in the straight line and together apologized for the last time, which could melt his ego.

"Disperse, don't make noise while going! Principal just passed away" replied the teacher. We laughed out loud within ourselves.

• • •

My journey with my Master, whom some referred to as a mere walk, was an adventure every day. It was another sunlit day, and I took my Master along the winding road. Would he impart new wisdom, or should I share my newfound knowledge with him? No matter what we did, what mattered was that we were together. Since yesterday, I have grown even more enamoured with my Master.

As we strolled down the familiar street, we came across a young boy walking his dog. The animal looked fierce yet magnificent, intimidating yet impressive, with its glossy fur, sturdy build, deadly claws and razor-sharp fangs. The boy appeared younger than me, but the dog exuded an air of power that made me feel inferior. I yearned for such a companion, one that could boost my confidence and elevate my social status. However, it was an expensive breed, and I could only afford to admire it from afar.

Suddenly, the dog pulled away from the boy, whose strength was no match for it. The animal sprinted towards a group of small children playing in a nearby park. The children scattered, but the dog leaped on one, clamping its teeth on the child's thigh and tearing away a chunk of flesh as if biting into a chicken burger. Blood gushed out, and the child howled in agony. The park keeper intervened, wrestling the dog away from the wounded child and dragging it off. The child was taken to the hospital, and the scene was terrifying.

Earlier, I was enticed by the idea of owning a dog that could enhance my social status. But as I witnessed the savagery of the animal and the boy's incapacity to handle it, I gradually began to understand that my Master was all I needed. He was my rock, my wellspring of knowledge and my true companion. It became clear to me that power without the ability to control it was a recipe for disaster, and I made a promise to myself to steer clear of such temptations. In the end, it was better to stay grounded and content with what I had than to seek out power and invite chaos into my life.

• • •

CHAPTER II

The Last Bench At School

At school, the last bench was more than just a place to sit. It was like a sanctuary for the lazy and the mischievous. A place of freedom, where we could daydream, pass notes, and crack jokes without fear of being caught. It was a place where friendships were forged, and memories were made that would last a lifetime.

The first benchers looked at us with disdain, as if we were a bunch of rebels with no cause. We were seen as the troublemakers who refused to conform to the norms. And the teachers? They had eyes everywhere, even at the back of their heads. But we had our ways. We had our secret stash of candies and energy drinks. We had our friends who would give us a heads-up when the teacher was approaching. Yes, being in the last bench was like being in a secret society. We had our own rules, our own rituals, and our own secret language. And if anyone dared to disturb our peace, we would unite like a pack of wolves. Well, maybe not wolves, more like a pack of sleepy cats. But you get the idea.

Arvind entered the classroom and took a seat beside me. He was like a firecracker, lighting up the room with his sparkling personality.

As I greeted him with a friendly "Hi, Arvind!", he raised his palm, signaling for a high-five with excitement.

"What's up? How was your weekend?" I asked him.

"It was great, bro. Do you know about this search engine from the US called Google? You can literally search anything on the web just by typing," replied Arvind with enthusiasm.

"Oh, that's great. People in the US are really into these technologies." I replied not knowing what else to say about Google

"Yes, I'm in love with it."

"Hmmm! Why can't our country also create such products?" I asked, with slight disappointment and a little curiosity.

"Because our country is busy creating people who create such products" Arvind laughed at his own joke.

I forgot all about Aravind as Miss Rashmi, our new biology teacher gracefully entered the classroom, my world stopped. She was the epitome of beauty and every boy in the room was entranced by her. Time seemed to slow down as she made her way to the blackboard, and I couldn't take my eyes off her. She had long, flowing hair that shimmered in the sunlight and soft, delicate features that seemed to glow from within. Her eyes were a bright shade of blue, with long eyelashes that fluttered as she blinked. She was like an enchantress, radiating beauty and poise in her elegant sari. I was in awe, and my heart was racing with excitement. Suddenly, I saw the injustice of my position in the last bench and cursed those lucky enough to be sitting in the front. How I longed to be closer, to bask in the radiance of this breath-taking woman. "I must sit in the front row from now on," I vowed to myself, determined to get as close to this heavenly creature as possible.

• • •

From teachers to parents and relatives, everyone had instilled the idea that this stage of my life was the most crucial, requiring me to study from sunrise to sunset and even beyond. I was frantically studying early in the morning, my mind racing with all the information I had to remember. But no matter how many times I read those lessons, the fear of forgetting everything on the day of the exam loomed over me like a dark cloud. It was as if my brain was betraying me, refusing to retain anything despite my best efforts.

Why was it so hard? Why couldn't I just understand and remember everything for once and for all? The desperation grew with every passing moment, as I realized that my future depended on these exams.

I wished it were as easy as just studying once, but it wasn't. I had to keep reading, re-reading, and re-re-reading until my eyes ached and my brain felt like it was about to explode. I longed to escape the suffocating routine of studying and spend time outside with my Master, who always had a way of teaching me valuable lessons in a way that made sense to me.

The morning was delightful and refreshing, and as I stood gazing up at the towering trees, I couldn't help but feel a sense of awe and wonder. The way the trees stood so tall, their branches reaching up to the sky, was a sight to behold. I marveled at their sheer size and beauty, wondering how such incredible structures could grow so effortlessly from the ground.

As I gazed in wonder at the trees, a question arose in my mind: what could be the secret behind their growth and how could they grow so high? Meanwhile, I couldn't help but feel a sense of smallness and insignificance compared to these majestic giants. Despite my feelings of inadequacy, I continued to gaze in awe at the trees, trying to fathom the mystery of their existence.

Suddenly, an epiphany struck me, like a bolt of lightning from the blue. The secret behind the tree's success lay in their deep roots, which kept them grounded even as they reached new heights. I was filled with a renewed sense of wonder and amazement at the intelligence of nature and the mysteries of life.

I was standing on the very same road where my dear friend had met with a fatal accident a year ago. A tempo traveler had run over her body, and the scene still haunted me like a nightmare. I vividly remembered how I had cried my heart out that day and how I couldn't sleep for an entire week. I had been utterly devastated and sunk into deep depression, refusing to talk to anyone. All I wanted was to be left alone with her memories, but her absence had made it even more unbearable.

As time passed, people said that I had recovered and returned to my normal life. However, deep down, I knew that the pain was still there, buried under the facade of normalcy. And now, here I was, standing on the very same spot where I had lost my beloved friend. The pain had simply transformed into something else, something more bearable, but the love remained just as strong.

Feeling lost and helpless, I turned to my Master and looked into his eyes, searching for comfort and solace amidst the overwhelming grief.

A few moments ago, I pondered on why I couldn't retain information for a lifetime by just reading it once. An impeccable memory could rob us of happiness. Life is a vessel brimming with problems, and if we could remember every one of them, we would never be able to find joy. Thankfully, there is a force in nature that helps us forget things, allowing us to move forward. If we wish to hold onto memories, constant revision is key. How wonderful it is to have this power in our hands, the ability to choose what memories to hold on to and what to let go of.

• • •

The following day, I returned from school after attending a workshop on "Go Green". We were attending a "Go Green" workshop, and I found myself dozing off during the speeches on vegetarianism. The vegetarians were all about being eco-friendly and treating animals kindly, while the non-vegetarians were raving about the delicious taste of meat and the nutrients it provides. The vegetarians boasted about how their diet results in ecological harmony, while the non-vegetarians' diet results in the destruction of life on the planet. It was like watching a boxing match, with each side delivering a blow after blow of their own arguments. But instead of joining in on the brawl, I chose to sit back and observe from the sidelines. I let out a few yawns and stretched my arms, waiting for the bell to ring. It was definitely not the most productive day at school, but it was certainly entertaining.

After returning home from school, my mom had asked me to pick up some chicken from the market, so I quickly freshened up and headed out with my Master. As we walked, I couldn't shake off the discussion we had back in school - the debate on vegetarianism was still ringing in my head. As we passed by a temple, we witnessed a priest scolding an old woman and verbally abusing her. It was heartbreaking to hear such disrespecting words coming from someone who chants auspicious Vedic mantras. We soon found out that the lady had forgotten to pay for a pooja. It made me wonder how a small oversight like that could lead to such misbehaviour from someone who is supposed to be a spiritual guide.

As I walked back from the market with a kilogram of chicken, my furry companion, Master, could not contain his excitement. His constant sniffing of the package was a clear indication of his hunger. I couldn't help but feel a pang of sadness as I thought about the bungalow owner who probably never fed the poor little dog. Unable to resist, I gave him a small piece of meat, and his eyes lit up with gratitude as he happily wagged his tail. It was at that moment that I realized the point of the debate we had been having in school that day comparing priest and Master's behaviour: it's not just about what goes into our mouth, but also what comes out of it.

My mom's chicken curry that night was a welcome distraction from the day's events, and as I savored each delicious bite, without any sense of guilt.

• • •

I gazed at the bungalow where my Master was always tied up. I couldn't help but wonder about the mysterious man who lived there. Who was the owner of that eerie house? Nobody seemed to know what went on inside those walls. Some claimed it was haunted, while others whispered of three murders that had taken place there. There was something peculiar and abnormal about the man who lived in that bungalow. People rarely saw him, and when they did, they quickly averted their eyes and went on their way. Those who had seen him before described him as having scars on his face, a hunchback, a limp, and cigarette burns on his hands and legs. Rumor had it that a family lived there twenty years ago, and one day the man's wife, brother-in-law, and mother-in-law were all killed inside the house. Since then, the man had lived alone in the bungalow, and everyone in the neighborhood was afraid of him. He never turned on his lights at night and rarely left his house. I had only seen him once before, when he was carrying some vegetables from the market. I couldn't help but notice a small knife sticking out of a hole in his pocket. He looked horrible, fearsome, wicked, and very dangerous.

As I stood there, my mind was consumed with worry for my dear Master. What fate could befall him in the clutches of that wicked man? How could one trust a man who may have committed unspeakable crimes? My heart raced as I comprehended that my Master could never be safe in that place. I had to act quickly, I had to save him. Losing yet another friend was not an option, especially when my Master reminded me of someone so special, someone who I believed to be the incarnation of my love.

With these thoughts racing through my mind, I hurriedly rushed out to check on Master. But to my dismay, he was nowhere to be found. Had the old man taken him out? Fear and panic started to grip me as I frantically searched for my furry friend. Oh, God! I pleaded, please show me a way to save my Master from the clutches of that evil man.

• • •

Life felt like a never-ending cycle of monotony - the same old school, the same old place, and the same old people with their mocking gazes. Instead of going to school, I chose to sit by the tranquil riverside and lose myself in the memories of my dear friend who was no longer with me.

We used to explore different places, spending hours by this very spot, pouring our hearts out to each other. Those moments were truly magical and etched in my memory forever. I eagerly waited to go to school every day, just to catch up with her. Back then, even the mundane routine of school felt like heaven. Being with her was a joy in itself - discussing the world and its wonders was always an enriching experience. When you're with the ones you love, even being confined in a cage feels like a blessing. You simply don't care about where you are or what might happen next.

Exactly one year ago, the sun was shining brightly, the birds were chirping happily, and the world seemed so alive - just like we did.

"You look good with your new T-shirt," she said, admiringly.

But of course, I couldn't let that slide without a bit of playful banter. "It is not that way you see, the T-shirt is looking good because I am wearing it! If I remove it, it will lose its beauty," I teased her.

She laughed and rolled her eyes. "Oh! That's very boastful. By the way, let me read what is written on it."

"Yeah sure," I replied, feeling amused.

"Every morning, I look into the mirror to see if I am handsome. But at the end of the day, all that matters is whether my day was awesome," she read aloud with a grin on her face.

"How is the quote?" I asked.

"It is awesome on a handsome guy," she chuckled.

I couldn't help but laugh along with her.

"That's what's adding beauty to the shirt," she said with a smile.

"The evening is so calm and serene with so many butterflies fluttering around," I observed.

"Would you mind if I tell you a story?" she asked.

"Not at all. I'm all ears," I replied, intrigued.

"But first, you have to catch a butterfly for me," she said, pointing to a colorful butterfly sipping nectar from a nearby flower.

"That's a challenge, but I'm up for it," I said confidently.

As I tiptoed towards the butterfly, trying not to scare it away, my inner child was bursting with excitement at the thought of catching the colorful creature. Just as I was about to grab it, the tricky little butterfly took off, fluttering gracefully from one flower to another. Determined to catch it, I chased the butterfly for what felt like an eternity. At one point, I even thought that catching girls was easier than this elusive butterfly. When I was almost on the verge of catching it, I slipped and fell into a swamp, covered in mud and shame. She laughed heartily, and I couldn't help but cry in embarrassment and frustration.

Beautiful things are not so easy to catch, my friend" she said.

"Whatever! I will be happy if you don't tell anyone about this incident." I replied.

"Hahaha" she laughed and agreed with a nod.

While I sat there lost in my memories, someone suddenly shook me out of my reverie. It was my friend David, and he was amused by my daydreaming. "Hi dude! What are you doing?" he asked with a smile.

I joked back, "I was just dreaming about you being the Prime Minister of India." We both laughed heartily before heading home together.

• • •

The next evening, I pedaled my way to Gopesh's surprise birthday party. Though I didn't particularly enjoy birthday celebrations, I was excited. After all, it wasn't every day that we got to dress up and mingle with the class girls, who always looked so lovely in their colorful outfits. I grinned as I checked myself out in the reflection of a passing car, feeling quite dapper in my favorite blue shirt and black jeans.

As I cycled past the Old man's bungalow, I caught sight of Master, chomping away on a leather piece and looking quite pleased with himself. Suddenly, I noticed the bungalow owner sprinting towards me with his face shrouded in a cloth. For a moment, I was taken aback, but then I shook it off. Who had time to worry about strange happenings when there was a party to attend and girls to impress? With that thought in mind, I pedaled even faster, eager to get to the celebration before the other guys showed up and stole all the attention.

At a distance, near Raju's ice cream shop, I spotted a crowd, and my curiosity was piqued. Was it an accident? A fight? Or just a group of people gawking at something interesting? As I hurried closer to see what had happened, my heart started racing with a sense of unease. A guy from a motorcycle had fallen with his leg and head wounded. People were discussing and investigating the incident rather than helping the poor wounded guy who wasn't even able to stand.

I got down from my cycle to help the bleeding man, a strange feeling washed over me. The elders who had gathered stopped me and were asking the man to lodge a complaint first, but something in their eyes told me they knew more than they were letting on. "Hell with the complaint! Can't you see? He is bleeding!" I yelled at them, growing more suspicious by the minute.

"The bungalow freak might have pelted stones at this man while he was on the bike. His madness is going out of the limits these days," the ice cream shop guy was commenting. Probably he might have seen.

Swami Uncle, who lived near the ice cream shop, exclaimed, "He's a psycho! If we don't take serious action now, we'll never know what else he'll do to the people in the colony." I tended to the wounded man's leg. I led him to a chair in the ice cream shop where Raju kindly offered him a glass of water. As he sipped it slowly, I could sense his unease and fear. "Please, let's forget about this," he said with a trembling voice. "I already feel a little better. I don't want to file a complaint against that bungalow man. I don't want to be haunted!"

The bungalow man was a source of fear for everyone in the colony. His erratic behavior and violent outbursts had caused much harm already, and I knew it was only a matter of time before he struck again. Even though I was getting late to the party, I rode my way back to check on my Master. I couldn't shake off the fear that gripped me. It was a relief when I found him still chewing on his leather piece, but as I looked around, I noticed something odd. There were several stones scattered around him. Could it have been the bungalow man who had thrown them? In a moment of desperation to protect, I picked up one of the stones and hurled it as high as I could into the sky, hoping that it would somehow provide a shield of protection for my beloved Master before it inevitably plummeted back down to the ground.

• • •

After a tiring day at school, I returned home and switched on the TV to watch a repeat telecast of a boring reality show, where reality is the least of their concerns. I found it more entertaining than the melodrama of the saas-bahu serials that the girls in my class incessantly discuss during break time. !

Craving a snack, I asked my mom to make me a sandwich, and she prepared it while passing comments on my academic performance. "You're so careless, just look at the marks you scored in the last exam. Even if you add up the marks from all subjects, it doesn't exceed a hundred," she continued to blabber on.

Indeed, my mother's words struck a chord of truth. Reflecting upon my recent academic performance, I couldn't deny the lack of genuine interest that plagued me during those fateful examinations. The memory of my dear departed friend loomed over me, a constant reminder of the void left in my life. We had been study companions for years, navigating the labyrinth of knowledge together, and now her absence was an insurmountable hurdle.

In all fairness, I had never been a complete slouch when it came to academics. However, the weight of grief had eroded my motivation. My scores, once respectable, plummeted to the depths of mediocrity, shattering the remaining shards of respect I held within the academic realm.

My mother's voice echoed through the room, a torrent of disapproval and frustration. "We sacrifice so much for you," she lamented, "fulfilling your every desire, only to be met with disappointment and anguish. Nowadays, all you do is waste away in front of that mindless box, flipping through channels as if it were a grand endeavor. Look at Anu auntie's son, how he excels. Learn from his example." Her words, like an unrelenting tide, crashed upon my ears, drowning any defense I may have mustered. In moments like these, the inanimate objects of the room become my silent confidants. The furniture, the floor, the ceiling offered solace, a respite from the barrage of words, incapable of launching verbal assault like a live machine gun.

After devouring the sandwiches, filled with tear-inducing onions, bleeding tomatoes, and spices as fiery as my mom's scoldings, I couldn't help but ponder. For a fleeting moment, I entertained the idea that even a brinjal sandwich would taste superior in comparison. As I stayed home longer, my mom's scoldings grew more frequent and intense. To escape, I decided to step outside and take a breath of fresh air.

I approached the old man's bungalow and noticed my Master sitting idly, seemingly just as bored as I was. It was one of the few pleasant aspects about the bungalow man - his tendency to rarely venture outside during the day. This granted me abundant time to bond with my Master. With great enthusiasm, I whisked him away from the walls of the bungalow, and together we embarked on a leisurely stroll along the bustling streets.

Every step I took down that road filled me with a profound sense of significance. The path was adorned with majestic Gulmohar trees,their vibrant blooms stretching out on either side, painting the surroundings with shades of fiery red. It was a sight that stirred a deep-rooted nostalgia within me, reminiscent of a time when my lost friend and I had strolled along this very road. I could vividly recall her enchantment with those crimson flowers, her eyes sparkling with delight as she admired their beauty. In that moment, as I walked amidst the Gulmohar trees, I couldn't help but feel a deep connection to her, as if her spirit lingered in the midst of those captivating blossoms.

I carefully picked one of the fallen Gulmohar flowers from the ground and presented it to her with a gentle smile. Her eyes lit up as she accepted it, appreciating its delicate beauty. "You might have been a fallen one," she remarked, "but you are the chosen one!" Her words carried a profound meaning, revealing her ability to find beauty and significance in even the simplest of things.

Caught in the moment, she looked at me and posed a thought-provoking question, "What do you want to become when you grow up?" Her inquiry delved into the realm of dreams and aspirations, inviting me to contemplate my future path.

"Hahaha you're the first person to ask me this question," I chuckled. "Most people just see me as a spoiled brat and don't bother with such sensible inquiries."

She raised an eyebrow, challenging my statement. "Mamatha ma'am asked us the same question this morning in school, didn't she? Have you already forgotten?" she questioned my memory, a mischievous glint in her eyes. Deep down, I couldn't help but smile at the mention of that lovely teacher.

"Oh yeah, you got me there," I admitted with a playful tone. "So maybe you're the second person to ask"

"I also remember an elderly person who came for inspection to our school last week asked the same question to you," she reminded me, showcasing her impressive memory. I couldn't help but marvel at her ability to recall such details.

"Ohh yeah, maybe you're right. So you're the third person then," I replied, adding one more to the count, an easier one compared to trigonometry.

Her laughter filled the air, contagious and joyful. "When you don't even remember the people who ask about your ambitions, how can you have your own passions?" her words hitting home with a touch of truth.

I smiled warmly at her. "I love the way you speak such bitter truth," I confessed, appreciating her candidness and genuine nature.

"I too love the way you come up with sweet lies," she mocked me, her words tinged with amusement.

I chuckled at her remark and decided to turn the tables. "So tell me, what do you want to be?" I asked, throwing her own question back at her.

Her expression turned slightly mischievous. "If you've forgotten, I asked you first, my friend," she replied, reminding me of our earlier conversation.

I thought for a moment, considering my aspirations. "Well, to be honest, my dreams keep changing. When I see a doctor saving lives, I want to be a doctor. When I watch Sachin Tendulkar play cricket, I dream of being a cricketer like him. But when I see terrorists... When I see terrorists..." I stumbled over my words, hesitating to continue.

She leaned in, her eyes filled with curiosity. "Go on, when you see terrorists?" she urged.

A mischievous smile crossed my face. "I feel like being at home, eating my mom's sandwich which tastes like terror on bread," I proclaimed, adopting a dramatic tone. We both burst into laughter, sharing the joy of our lighthearted banter.

"You must be kidding about your last dream," she remarked, still smiling from our shared laughter.

No. Not at all. I am as serious as Charlie Chaplin on the screen."

"Be like Einstein and answer seriously." She frowned.

"Do you know what is common between those two personalities ?" I asked.

"Chaplin had a weird moustache and Einstein had weird hair." She said looking at my messy hair.

"You are very funny," I said, adjusting my hair.

"You tell me, what else do you think is common between a comedian and a genius?'" she replied

"Once Einstein applauded Chaplin saying that, one of the most admirable features about his acting is, it is universal. Everybody, the young, the old, the deaf and the dumb, whoever watched him could understand him."

"That's true," she said, looking amazed.

"Then Chaplin replied to Einstein saying that though nobody understands your contribution completely, yet everyone admires it."

"Beautiful. I always wonder why great personalities vary so much and yet the world respects them. What is that one thing that makes them successful? Isn't it wonderful?" She seemed lost in her beautiful thoughts again.

"Yeah, okay, now it's your turn. Tell me about your dream," I reminded her.

"Cop," she said.

"Then I will become a cop too!" I exclaimed, jumping in front of her with sudden excitement. However, she remained silent and didn't react. I sensed a heaviness in her heart.

"I can never be a cop," she said softly, her voice filled with sorrow, as she looked down at her missing leg, silently bearing all her pain.

"No, you can. You will. I promise you," I consoled her without a second thought.

As the van sped by, its rush of air jolting me back to reality, I realized the weight of my promise. My Master, who sat before me with unwavering loyalty and trust, deserved nothing less than my utmost dedication. Her dream of becoming a cop, a dream she couldn't fulfil herself, now rested in my hands.

With a newfound determination, I looked into Master's eyes, searching for any hint of reassurance. I could almost see a spark of hope, a glimmer of belief that her dream could still come true.

"I will make it happen, Master," I affirmed, my voice filled with conviction. "Together, we will find a way." Master's tail wagged in response, a gesture of unwavering faith and unconditional love. It was a silent agreement between us, a bond forged in determination and a shared purpose.

• • •

It was getting late for school. I had made a promise to my friend Kiran, so called Fatso, that I would wait for him near the park, our usual meeting spot. I had spent the entire night pondering on how to train my Master, so I ended up oversleeping. Despite my Mom's melodious morning complaints, I couldn't bring myself to eat the delicious breakfast. I decided to skip it and quickly rode my bicycle to the park.

Filled with worry over my friend's potential scolding, I hastened my pace to reach our designated meeting spot.

However, upon arrival, my friend was nowhere to be found. I assumed that he must have already departed for school, considering the lateness of the hour. Engulfed in self-blame for my carelessness, I suddenly spotted Fatso hurrying towards me, his enthusiasm surpassing even my own. "Goodness gracious! This guy is crazier than I am," I thought to myself, and hastened my steps to meet him.

"Sorry for being late, bro," Fatso, my cherished and irreplaceable friend, offered his sincere apology. In his left hand, he carried two bananas and an orange, while his right hand grasped a generously-sized Tiffin box.

"Didn't you have breakfast? You seem to be carrying a lot of food for lunch break," I inquired.

"I had only eight idlis, Rahul! I was running late, so I grabbed these fruits, just in case I get hungry on the way to school," he replied, his words somewhat muffled by the half-eaten banana in his mouth.

"Would you mind sharing some with me? I skipped my breakfast as I was running late and didn't want to keep you waiting," I said, adopting an innocent expression.

"Oh, sure, bro! How long have you been waiting?" he asked, ready to share his bounty.

"I actually arrived a while ago, Fatso. It's been 35 minutes. I was bored out of my mind," I lied.

"Oh, really? My bad, bro. Sorry about that. Let's not waste any more time. We can chat on the way," he replied apologetically.

"Yeah, you're right. Mamatha ma'am won't let us in if we're late. I don't want to miss it," I chuckled. He handed me half a banana and apologized once again for being late.

"No worries, Fatso. Waiting wasn't difficult for me. After all, you're my lifesaver," I reassured him, hoping to flatter him and perhaps get another piece of food. He handed me half an orange, and I quickly devoured it before he could ask for it back.

"Fatso, do you happen to know anyone who trains dogs or has knowledge about them?" I inquired.

"I know a man who runs a circus with a monkey near my house. Maybe he could help you," Fatso responded, offering an unhelpful suggestion.

"Hmm," I sighed with disappointment.

"By the way, I know someone who knows a lot about animals, he is my father's friend" Fatso exclaimed, bringing a ray of hope. "I don't really understand what that man says, but maybe he can help you. I'll get you his details."

"Wow!" I exclaimed, filled with excitement.

"He lives about two kilometers from here, in Vivek Nagar. I'll give you the exact details tomorrow," Fatso promised.

"Fatso, you're truly my best buddy. Just name it, and I'll make it happen," I flattered him.

He then handed me a hidden banana from the secret compartment of his lunch basket. Fatso and I entered the classroom, munching on an apple he had concealed in his pocket.

• • •

The last bench was my favorite spot in the classroom, and I had Arvind sitting next to me. In recent weeks, it seemed as though his enthusiasm had dimmed. It was as if someone had cast a spell on him, draining him of all his energy and spark. His eyes, once filled with mischief, now looked lost in thought, as if pondering over a grave secret. He had once confided in me about the pressure of studies getting to him. It was a crucial phase, after all, with board exams looming on the horizon. But the last bench was supposed to be a place of respite, a haven for those who needed a break from the monotony of academics. Maybe, Arvind needed more than just a break. As I greeted him with a friendly "Hi Arvind!", his lacklustre response left me even more curious.

"What was going on with him?" I thought to myself and ignored it.

While attendance, lectures, assignments, and notes filled the classroom, our minds were occupied with countless thoughts and unimaginable dreams. With my cheek resting on my palm, my eyes fixated on the blackboard, and my hands and legs restless, I pondered over the events that had unfolded.

It was nearly a year and a half ago. The air was electric with anticipation as the semifinal match of the state-level Inter-school cricket tournament reached its climax. Our school had never tasted victory in the cricket championship, and this was our chance to change that. The situation was intense, and the stakes couldn't have been higher.

With just one run needed to secure our triumph, and only one ball remaining, it was my turn to face the challenge. The crowd erupted into a frenzy, their voices reverberating through the stadium, as they chanted my name in unison. But this wasn't an ordinary moment. It wasn't just about adding another run to the score. This was personal.

You see, I hadn't reached 99 runs; this was my very first ball. Earlier in the match, while fielding, I had suffered a hamstring injury that forced me to retire hurt. The pain was excruciating, and my left leg had lost its stability. Running was out of the question; I could only limp. But there was no other choice. I was the last batsman standing, and it all came down to this one run from one ball.

In that pivotal moment, with one run needed and one ball remaining, I stood alone on the cricket pitch. Even though the match was drawn, we would not qualify for the finals as the opposite team had a better net run rate. The rules forbade me from having a runner, so it was up to me to make that crucial dash of 22 yards. The pressure was immense, but I was determined to give it my all.

The bowler standing at the other end was a formidable opponent, perhaps one of the best in all the teams. He had displayed his prowess by taking five wickets earlier in the match, and his reputation as one of the most accurate bowlers in the state preceded him. Despite his skill, he was also known for his sportsmanship and friendly nature. I remembered asking him once how he managed to bowl with such precision, to which he replied with a modest shrug, "I don't know."

As I faced him now, the weight of the moment was almost unbearable. How did I feel in that instant? If someone were to ask me, my answer would mirror the bowler's response—I don't know. Emotions churned within me like a tempest, a mix of nervousness, excitement, and a glimmer of hope. The next few seconds would determine the outcome of the match and could potentially change the course of our team's journey.

As the bowler embarked on his run-up, determination etched on his face, I braced myself for the imminent clash between bat and ball. With every stride, he propelled himself forward, his focus unwavering. I readied my stance, anticipating the delivery that would define the fate of our team's journey to the finals. The ball left the bowler's hand, hurtling towards me with pace and precision. It swung in the air, veering dangerously close to my stumps. In that fleeting moment, I made my move, attempting to connect bat to ball. But fate had a different plan. The ball darted through the gap between my bat and my legs, crashing into the stumps with a resounding thud. I stood frozen in disbelief, my hopes shattered in an instant. It was a perfect yorker, an unplayable delivery that left me defenceless.

I couldn't bring myself to lift my head, as the weight of disappointment bore down upon me. Emotions swirled within, a mixture of frustration and acceptance. There were no tears, no smiles, just a lingering silence as the opposition team erupted in celebration. Their victory had been sealed, and the realization washed over me like a bitter wave. The dream of reaching the finals had slipped through our grasp, replaced by the triumph of our opponents. The sound of cheers and jubilation filled the air, contrasting sharply with the silent disappointment that engulfed our team.

With a surge of disbelief and newfound hope, I lifted my head, only to witness a sight that defied all expectations. The umpire's arm was extended, signalling a no-ball. A rush of exhilaration coursed through my veins, instantly transforming the atmosphere. The tide of celebration had shifted, and it was our team's turn to revel in the moment. The field erupted with excitement as players rushed towards me, their footsteps echoing with triumphant cheers. At that moment, I felt like a superhero, basking in the unexpected turn of events. I anticipated being hoisted upon my teammates' shoulders, hailed as the savior of our team.

But my euphoria was short-lived. As my teammates surrounded me, it became clear that their objective wasn't to lift me in celebration. They came not to applaud my valiant effort but to retrieve the wickets and seize the victory that had eluded us moments ago. Their focus had shifted from my role in the game to securing the win.

I stood there, caught between conflicting emotions. The elation of a reprieve and the sudden realization that my personal triumph had been overshadowed by the pursuit of victory. No one seemed to take notice of my injured leg, nor did they spare a thought for the emotions coursing through me. Disheartened, I made my way back to the pavilion, my limp a stark reminder of the challenges I had faced. How foolish I had been to hope for praise and recognition for my zero on the scorecard.

As I stood there, lost in my own thoughts and disappointment, a girl approached me. Her presence caught me by surprise.

"Well done," she said, her voice filled with sincerity and understanding.

"Thanks, but I didn't do anything at all. I just got out on a duck," I replied, my tone tinged with self-deprecation.

She looked at me with empathy in her eyes, her words carrying a weight of wisdom beyond her years. "Never mind. It takes a lot of strength to play with such a limping leg. Trust me, I know."

"Thank you". I smiled faintly looking at her one leg. That was the first time I met Her.

The sound of the bell for lunch break brought me back to reality, and I was back to my senses. Fatso, always one step ahead, had already started unpacking his Tiffin box, unleashing an enticing aroma of Dosa that filled the air.

. . .

CHAPTER III

Be(aware) Of Dogs

That weekend, I embarked on a bicycle ride to meet the zoologist, who happened to be a friend of Fatso's father. He was known for his passion for wildlife and his deep understanding of animal evolution. According to Fatso, he would be available at six in the evening on Saturdays, as the rest of his week was dedicated to exploring and studying the Earth's lost creatures.

As the sun began to set, casting a beautiful twilight glow, the birds started their journey back to their nests. Streetlights illuminated the surroundings, creating a warm ambiance, while the aroma of chai and freshly fried bajjis wafted through the air along the roadside.

Finally, I reached the designated location. Hanging on the gate was a wooden sign that immediately caught my attention: 'Alexander.' It was the name I had been given as the contact person. However, my gaze shifted to another signboard nearby, which warned, 'Beware of dogs.' Here I was, to get "Aware of dogs", but the signboard warned, "Beware of dogs". I couldn't help but reflect on the irony of seeking knowledge about dogs while being cautioned about them.

There he stood, opening the gate with a friendly smile. In his hand, he held a magnificent golden retriever who was brimming with energy. The dog's excitement was palpable as it approached me, sniffing curiously as if I were an intriguing stranger. For a brief moment, doubt crossed my mind, and I wondered if I was truly capable of training a dog. Fear gripped me, but Alexander reassured me, saying,

"Don't worry, kid. He's just getting to know you." With his reassurance, I mustered the courage to step inside.

As I entered, I was greeted by the sight of a grand bungalow with a sprawling garden. A small fountain adorned the center, where water gracefully arched through the air. The lush green lawn was meticulously maintained, and peculiar plants added a touch of uniqueness to the surroundings. We settled under a shady tree, where a couple of bamboo chairs awaited us. A maid appeared, carrying a tray with steaming coffee and a few biscuits. Alexander kindly offered them to me, and I gratefully accepted, savoring the warmth of the drink and the sweet taste of the biscuits.

"So, how are you, Rahul?" he asked with familiarity, as if we were old acquaintances.

"I'm doing great, sir. Thank you. And how about you?" I replied, making sure to sound polite and composed.

"Call me Alex. I'm doing just fine, kid. So, tell me, what brings you here?" he inquired, his tone filled with genuine curiosity.

"I have a dog, and I want to train it to be as impressive as the dogs I see on TV shows," I explained.

"That's wonderful. So, you want to train your dog," he affirmed.

"Yes, I want to make him a cop," I said eagerly.

"Haha, you're quite innocent. While you can't exactly make it a cop, you can definitely train it to be a police dog that helps in uncovering hidden secrets," Alex explained, a hint of amusement in his voice.

"Yes!" I replied with enthusiasm.

"So, why do you want to train your dog and make it a police dog?" Alex asked, delving into the motivation behind my aspirations.

"I don't really know. I just love being with my dog, and I want to give something back to my Master," I answered honestly.

"Nice, very nice indeed," he smiled, showing his genuine interest in my endeavor.

"I have no idea what to do or how to go about it. It would be amazing if you could help me, Alex," I pleaded, hoping for his guidance.

"You don't have to request so much, buddy! I'm convinced. I'm always happy to help, although I may be a bit busy with my work schedule at times," he reassured me.

"That's okay, Alex. I'm truly honored," I replied gratefully.

"By the way, what breed is your dog?" he inquired.

"It's a male German Shepherd," I answered.

"Great! You couldn't have asked for a better choice. German Shepherds are intelligent, agile, and fast," he began, but I interrupted him.

"But Alex..." I hesitated.

"What is it, Rahul?" he asked, sensing my uncertainty.

"It... it doesn't have a leg," I revealed.

"Oh! I'm sorry to hear that, Rahul," he said sympathetically.

"Will I still be able to train it like other dogs?" I asked, seeking reassurance.

"Oh, absolutely! There is always something beyond legs, hands, or eyes when it comes to training dogs," he assured me.

"Thank you. I'm so glad to hear that," I replied with a sense of relief and gratitude.

Alex's mobile phone rang, interrupting our conversation. He excused himself and stepped away to take the call. I patiently waited, observing the serene surroundings of the garden. After a minute, Alex returned with a slightly apologetic expression on his face.

"I'm sorry, Rahul. I have something important to attend to right now. Would it be alright for you to come tomorrow morning? It's Sunday, and I'll be free to give you all the tips and information you need to start training," he proposed.

"Oh, no problem at all, Alex. Tomorrow works perfectly for me. I'll see you then," I replied, accepting the change in plans. As we bid farewell, I couldn't resist grabbing two cream biscuits from the table as a little treat for myself on the way back.

• • •

My girl and I boarded a bus, embarking on a journey together. She expressed her desire to visit the market and requested my assistance. I suggested that I could go alone and procure everything she needed, allowing her to stay at home. However, she adamantly declined my offer. As the bus commenced its journey, we found ourselves seated side by side in the middle row.

"Thank you for sacrificing your cricket game to be with me," she expressed warmly, her voice filled with sweetness. I had initially planned to play cricket, but being by her side felt far more significant in that moment.

"Oh, my team will have a hard time without me, you know," I boasted playfully, flashing a grin.

"Ahem," she interjected, her tone turning sharp. "I still remember how many runs you scored in the semi-final match." Her comment caught me off guard, and I felt a surge of embarrassment wash over me.

"Oh, forget about the scores," I persisted in my self-praise. "When I'm there, it gives the team a lot of strength. I'm their lucky charm, carrying the burden of the team."

"Oh, please! Enough with your boasting," she retorted, her tone filled with exasperation. "Self-praise is no praise at all. Haven't you heard that before? Just imagine what could have happened if you had actually gotten out on that ball the other day."

"That's precisely why I claim to be the lucky charm. I have the power to make the opposition bowler deliver a no ball, you see," I replied with a chuckle.

"Hmmm," she sighed, clearly unconvinced by my playful explanation.

"Your extra finger is really cute" I said pointing at her hand which had a tiny extra finger next to her little finger.

"There's never anything extra in life, somebody's loss is someone's gain" she replied in a cryptic way, maybe suggesting that she has no leg, but an extra finger on her hand.

"So what is it that you wanted to buy?" I asked, hoping to shift the conversation and keep her talking. I always enjoyed hearing her speak about anything and everything.

"Books," she replied.

"Oh my God! How many more books do you need? You already have plenty of them," I exclaimed, feigning surprise.

"They're not for me," she clarified.

"Then?" I inquired, curious to know the purpose behind her book-shopping.

"For the kids in the orphanage," she replied. Her words struck me, and I fell silent for a moment. I knew her background story well. She had been raised in an orphanage ever since her parents passed away when she was a young child. Someone had extended a helping hand and facilitated her admission into our school, recognizing her intelligence and eagerness to learn. In addition to attending school during the day, she dedicated her evenings to teaching the other children in the orphanage. While many of us relied on our parents for

support, she had already taken it upon herself to assist and uplift other kids in need.

In the midst of the chaos, a commotion erupted in the bus. Two elderly men were engaged in a heated dispute over a seat, their voices rising and echoing through the crowded space. Some passengers attempted to intervene and defuse the situation, while others chose to ignore the altercation altogether. The bus was packed with people, and the argument unfolded a couple of rows ahead of us. I watched in silence, unsure of how to react.

To my surprise, she stood up from her seat and offered it to one of the elderly men. I couldn't comprehend her actions. How could she do that? The old man hurriedly took the seat without even acknowledging her gesture or expressing gratitude. Filled with anger, I rose from my seat, intending to confront him and make him aware of her disability. But before I could voice my frustration, she calmly urged me not to engage in an argument and reminded me that our stop was approaching.

As we stepped off the bus, a wave of astonishment washed over the passengers. They seemed oblivious to her absence amidst the chaos of the quarrel. Their eyes widened in surprise as they caught sight of her gracefully maneuvering her way down with the aid of her crutches. Even the elderly men who had been engaged in the dispute halted their argument and watched her in silent awe.

We made our way to the bookstore, and she proceeded to order a substantial stack of books. With a mischievous smile, she turned to me, her gaze expectant, as if anticipating my response to her unspoken request for assistance.

"Oh, me?" I asked incredulously, my eyes widening as I took in the sheer size of the pile before us.

"If I am not wrong, you are the strength of your team. You carry all the burden of your...?" she said in a mocking voice.

And we laughed heartily.

Gazing at the twinkling stars, memories of our time together flooded my mind. Each moment was etched vividly in my memory, as if it had unfolded just yesterday. The laughter, the conversations, the shared experiences—they all swirled together, creating a tapestry of cherished moments, before I fell asleep in the lap of the unknown.

• • •

The next morning, I woke up a bit earlier than usual, filled with anticipation for my meeting with Alex. As I left home, I glanced back at the old bungalow, but my Master was nowhere in sight. My determination to learn about dog training and free my Master from the clutches of that evil man grew stronger.

After a 20-minute ride, I arrived at Alex's place promptly at 8 AM. To my surprise, I found him in the garden, engaged in his morning exercises. The serene surroundings and the sight of Alex's dedication filled me with a sense of admiration and excitement for the day ahead.

"Good morning, Alex," I greeted him eagerly.

"Oh, rise and shine, huh? A jolly good morning to you, Rahul" he chimed in.

Alex suggested going for a jog in the nearby park instead of under the tree in his garden where the maid had magically appeared with a tray of coffee and biscuits yesterday. "Absolutely! I would love to join you for a jog," I replied, ready to embrace the opportunity to spend more time with him and learn from his expertise. The prospect of jogging alongside Alex, discussing dogs and training, filled me with anticipation.

As we walked towards the park, I couldn't help but notice the golden retriever happily trotting alongside us, its curious nose exploring every scent along the way. The weather was perfect, with a gentle breeze caressing our faces, and the coolness in the air rejuvenated my spirits. I tried not to think about the missed opportunity to enjoy some biscuits earlier, focusing instead on the adventure that awaited me in the park.

"So, how is your German Shepherd, Rahul?" he asked.

"It is doing just great—always cheerful and playing around," I replied, though I was a bit hesitant to tell the whole story.

"That's really nice."

As we reached the park and began to jog, I asked, "So, Alex, what is it that I should know about training dogs?"

"You seem to be in a hurry to start the training right away," Alex made fun.

I chuckled at Alex's remark. "Well, not exactly in a hurry, but I am eager to learn and make progress. I want to give my dog the best training possible."

Alex nodded understandingly. "That's a commendable attitude, Rahul. Before we dive into the training techniques, it's important to understand the fundamentals. Building a strong foundation is key to successful dog training."

As we continued jogging, Alex started explaining the basics of dog training. He emphasized the importance of positive reinforcement, consistency, and patience. He shared insights on understanding a dog's behavior, body language, and how to establish trust and bond with them.

He also discussed the significance of establishing clear communication through commands and cues, and the importance of rewarding desired behaviors rather than punishing unwanted ones. Alex stressed that training should be a positive and enjoyable experience for both the dog and the trainer.

"Why is it that dogs alone have the ability to identify thieves and find lost items? Why don't horses, cats, and other animals do the same?" I asked.

"That's a very interesting question. But before I answer that, let me tell you about their history—why man chose dogs, or perhaps why dogs chose man as companions," he said, as if to pique my curiosity further.

"Okay!"

"According to recent discoveries through the application of mitochondrial DNA analysis, wolves and dogs share a common ancestor. In simple words, dogs are descended from wolves," he began to explain.

"Wow!"

Though the whole DNA thing went over my head like a frisbee thrown by an Olympic champion, I managed to hold on to one important nugget of knowledge: our beloved furry companions, the dogs, are distant relatives of those majestic howlers, the wolves.

"So, are you saying that dogs and wolves are the same?" I asked.

"Yeah, that's right. There are indeed several similarities and dissimilarities between dogs and wolves. Both species possess acute senses of smell and hearing. They have teeth that are designed for seizing, slicing, and tearing rather than chewing. Additionally, domestic dogs, like their wolf ancestors, tend to follow the guidance of an alpha dog or dominant member in their pack."

I listened attentively to Alex's explanations, feeling like a child captivated by a ghost story. I was unsure of what to ask next, but Alex anticipated my curiosity and continued, "However, there are some notable differences as well. For instance, dogs bark, but wolves generally don't."

"Very interesting," I responded, fascinated by the world of dogs and wolves.

"Let me share even more intriguing facts with you. Long ago, possibly around 500 BC, wolves lived in packs much like prehistoric human communities. It's likely that these wolves and humans competed for a similar place in the food chain. They shared many predators and prey. In the earliest interactions between humans and wolves, it's possible that wolves observed and learned to follow cave men on hunts, feeding on the remains of the animals that the primitive humans managed to kill. It's equally plausible that the opposite might also have been true."

"So, you're saying that instead of being adversaries, they formed an alliance?" I inquired.

"Exactly. Humans possessed advanced reasoning abilities and intelligence, while wolves boasted speed, strength, and endurance. It seems that these two species were destined to combine their mental and physical capabilities to serve one another," Alex explained.

"Amazing!" I exclaimed, captivated by the incredible synergy between humans and wolves throughout history.

"Yes, for a dog to thrive alongside humans, it needed to recognize the human as the dominant or alpha member of its pack. The process of domestication likely began when wolf puppies were taken from their dens at an early age, raised, trained, and selectively bred by humans, eventually leading to the creation of domestic dogs."

"I will make my master the alpha member," I stated, as if lost in a trance.

"Master?" Alex questioned.

"Yes, I've named him 'Master'," I replied.

"That's sweet. But remember, when you're training, you need to take charge and be his master," Alex advised.

"Sure, I will," I affirmed.

"Come, let's head back now. I'll lend you a book on dog training," Alex offered.

If it had been a chemistry book, I would have complained, but this was different. I felt a surge of excitement.

• • •

As I prepared for another mundane Monday at school, the usual morning routine was disrupted by the piercing wails of an ambulance tearing through the quiet neighborhood. The urgency in its sound hinted at a dire situation unfolding nearby. Curiosity mingled with concern, compelling me to venture beyond the comfort of my home. Stepping outside, the atmosphere seemed charged with an eerie energy, as if the very air held secrets waiting to be unveiled. The police vans arrived swiftly, their sirens adding to the symphony of chaos. Determined to unravel the mystery, I mounted on my bicycle and followed the police vehicles.

Pedaling through familiar streets now tinged with an air of uncertainty, my eyes caught sight of Fatso, who is usually cheerful. Today, however, he appeared transformed, his usually plump frame diminished, and his gait resembling that of a restless wanderer. It seemed as though he had been traversing the boundaries of reality, lost in a realm only he could fathom. Hunger emanated from him, a palpable hunger that transcended mere physical nourishment, as if he hadn't savored sustenance in the past three days.

"Hey, Fatso. What's going on? Why are you wandering like this?" I asked, concerned about lacing my voice as I approached him cautiously. He appeared visibly horrified, his eyes darting around with a haunted expression. It was as if he didn't even recognize me, lost in the depths of his distress.

"Why, Fatso? What has terrified you so?" I inquired, my own anxiety mounting as his fear seemed to envelop me.

He struggled to speak, his words stumbling out in a jumble that I couldn't decipher. "David..." he managed to utter, his voice trembling.

My heart skipped a beat. "What happened to David?" I implored, my voice tinged with apprehension.

"David... murdered." he finally revealed, his words hanging heavily in the air.

"What?" The shock reverberated through every fibre of my being, momentarily leaving me speechless and unable to process the gravity of his words.

Trying to regain my composure, I pressed further. "What are you saying? Where did this happen? When? How?" The questions poured out of me, a torrent of confusion and disbelief overwhelming my senses.

"He had invited me to his house yesterday to play, as his parents were out of town. But I couldn't make it," Fatso continued, his voice trembling with guilt. "So, I thought I would drop by now, before school, to apologize for not coming. When I rang the doorbell, there was no response. The door was already open, so I entered. Calling out for him, I went to his room and... and found him lying on the floor. Lifeless."

His words hung heavy in the air, punctuated by his tears. I held him tightly, offering what little comfort I could amidst the overwhelming grief. The police vans had arrived near David's house, the scene now shrouded in an ominous air of tragedy.

"David's sister is nowhere to be found either," Fatso whispered, his voice filled with worry and uncertainty.

"Oh God," I uttered, a sense of profound sorrow gripping my heart. The weight of the situation pressed upon us, leaving us searching for answers and struggling to comprehend the magnitude of the loss that had befallen our dear friend.

· · ·

In the wake of the shocking events, the school administration had declared a holiday, acknowledging the unsettling circumstances that had unfolded. David's father, being a highly respected figure in the town, drew the attention and scrutiny of the police, intensifying their efforts in the murder investigation.

I attempted to immerse myself in the book Alex had given me, hoping for a distraction from the grim reality surrounding us. However, my mind remained restless and unable to focus, the words on the pages blurring together.

The following day, as I skimmed through the newspaper, my eyes caught a column dedicated to David and his missing sister, Elena, who was two years elder to him. The article revealed that the police had uncovered crucial information: Elena had been involved with a boyfriend named Matthew, a fellow student from her college. It was disclosed that she had recently ended their relationship. Furthermore, her new boyfriend had also gone missing, raising suspicions about their possible connection to the unfolding tragedy. In response, the police had assembled search teams to track down these individuals in the hopes of obtaining substantial evidence.

As I immersed myself in reading the newspaper, a distant voice called out from the gate, drawing my attention away from the article. Curiously, I made my way outside to investigate. To my surprise, it was Arjun, a fifth-grade kid from the neighboring street. He often visited our house to gather flowers for his mother's pooja. I couldn't help but wonder about his situation. If his mother dedicated her days to worship and performing rituals, who took care of this young boy? Moreover, Arjun's father had gone to Dubai in search of job and livelihood.

"Can I pluck a few flowers?" Arjun asked, his innocent eyes filled with hope.

"Of course, come in," I welcomed him, inviting him inside the gate.

As I watched him carefully select the flowers, my gaze wandered towards the eerie presence of the old bungalow nearby. A chilling sensation coursed through me, and a thought crossed my mind—could this mysterious, unsettling old man be somehow connected to David's tragic murder?

• • •

A week had elapsed since the harrowing murder had shaken our town, and the initial frenzy surrounding the incident was gradually subsiding. During this time, I had distanced myself from my Master, fearing the possibility of the bungalow man's involvement in the murder. The thought of risking our safety and involvement in the unfolding tragedy kept me at bay.

On a Saturday evening, seeking solace and respite from the turmoil that had enveloped our community, I made my way to the riverside. It was a place where I found solace, a sanctuary for reflection. Lost in my thoughts, I allowed myself to immerse in cherished memories of Her, my lost friend. The moments we had shared together played like a movie in my mind, each scene etched with beauty and joy.

"What is your favorite color?" she asked, her tone filled with skepticism.

"To be frank, I am color blind," I replied honestly.

"Liar! You always say such stupid things and are never serious," she retorted, refusing to believe my words.

It was frustrating. For once, I spoke the truth, and yet she doubted me like a criminal. I tried to explain, "No, really, I mean it. I struggle to differentiate between red and green or their mixtures. While I can perceive primary colors individually, once they are blended with others, I can't find the *difference. It's not a severe case, but it does pose challenges. That's why I dislike chemistry lab, where you have to identify subtle variations like reddish green versus reddish brown in those complex experiments." I sighed, feeling the weight of her disbelief.*

She chuckled, dismissing my explanation. "Haha. How clever. Now you're proving your lies with reasons too. I still don't believe you. You're just making up stories."

I felt defeated. There was no convincing her. It was like being a shepherd crying, "Fox, fox!" when the fox had actually arrived, but no one believed it. I gave up on trying to make her understand and decided to settle with lies.

"Hmmm. Blue is my favorite color," I fabricated, hoping to appease her.

"Nice. Good choice," she responded, seemingly satisfied with my answer. I couldn't help but wonder why people readily believed my lies while doubting my truths. It left me contemplating the nature of truth itself, questioning what it truly meant.

"So, which one is yours?" I asked, curious about her favorite color.

"The color of water," she replied with a smile.

"What? But water is colorless. How can that be your favorite color?" I asked, genuinely puzzled.

"Yes, that's precisely why it's my favorite. Isn't it beautiful? Can you think of anything else on this planet that is colorless and yet visible?" she questioned, reaching down to scoop up a handful of water from the river before returning it. Her eyes sparkled with joy, and she seemed genuinely happy appreciating the wonders of nature. I pondered her question for a moment but couldn't come up with a satisfactory answer.

"Indeed, it is spectacular," I admitted. As I spoke, thoughts of the colorless acids in the chemistry lab crossed my mind.

Hydrochloric acid, sulfuric acid—there were colorless substances I could mention to challenge her point. However, as I looked at her radiant face, I decided against it. It was better not to get into an argument, especially with someone as enchanting as her.

"The creation is truly beautiful," she exclaimed, clearly mesmerized.

"Yes, it is," I agreed.

We continued our walk along the riverside in comfortable silence, relishing the soothing sounds of the flowing river and the gentle breeze. After some time, I broke the silence and asked, "What do you like about me?"

"You don't share much of your feelings with others, but you do with me. I am a liar. What makes you choose me?" I asked, feeling a mix of vulnerability and curiosity.

"You may lie, but you don't mean it. There's something genuine about you, and I find that appealing. I enjoy every bit of our conversation," she replied with a warm smile, her eyes reflecting sincerity. I couldn't help but wonder how she managed to maintain such a radiant smile.

"So, you prefer a lie over the truth? Why does the world emphasize the importance of speaking the truth, yet you seem to appreciate my lies? What am I supposed to make of it? What exactly is truth, then?" I asked, feeling a bit unsettled. She seemed to sense the whirlwind of thoughts that had consumed me in that moment.

"Hmm, let me ask you a few questions before I answer," she proposed, and I remained silent, waiting for her to continue.

"Why does a mother say that her child is the most beautiful, even if the child is born handicapped? Why does a doctor assure a patient that they are strong, even if they have only a few days to live? Why does a friend console you by saying that everything will get better, even when there seems to be

no hope whatsoever?" she inquired, her voice gentle yet filled with profound meaning. A lie uplifts the weak more than the truth. A lie is beautiful when the truth is defeating. Why did freedom fighters speak the truth even though they ended up in jail many times? Why are you always awarded the marks you truly deserve, even though a little grace could land you in a better position? Even though a lie is an easier path, truth is more cherished in the long run. Sometimes a lie is beautiful, and sometimes truth stands above all. So, what do you follow? Though the words you speak can convince the whole world, will it convince yourself? Anything you speak, if you are one with it, if you are speaking the truth, no matter what it is to the world...!" she answered with eloquence, her words resonated deeply within me.

I was spellbound, at a loss for words. Her perspective on life and truth was truly remarkable. "Thank you," was all I could manage to say, overwhelmed by the depth of her insights.

"Now you know what you are," she said. No one had ever answered my queries in such a beautiful way as she had. While the whole world was busy finding faults, she was searching for beauty even in the lies.

Sitting on the rock near the river, I threw a stone into it and watched it pitch multiple times. If she was here, she would have answered why it did so.

• • •

I spent the rest of the week engrossed in the book, delving into the fascinating world of training German Shepherds. It provided a wealth of information, including captivating stories about their origins and distinctive traits. I was particularly intrigued by the tale of how these remarkable dogs earned their name. In ancient times, as humans transitioned from hunting to raising livestock for sustenance, the need arose for a vigilant companion to oversee and manage the growing herds. Wolves, with their sharp instincts, were tamed and transformed into shepherds, diligently protecting the sheep. Hence, these dogs became known as shepherds. As for the "German" in their name, it originated from their lineage being nurtured and developed in Germany. Renowned for their intelligence and trainability, German Shepherds found their place not only in herding and farming but also in important roles such as police work and military service.

Lost in these captivating facts, my thoughts drifted to my beloved Master. How did the enigmatic man in the bungalow come across Master? Why did Master have only three legs? Was it a birth defect, or had the sinister man inflicted harm upon him? A multitude of questions swirled in my mind, fuelling my determination to uncover the truth. Regardless of the circumstances, I knew in my heart that Master was meant to be by my side, and I would do whatever it took to protect and care for him.

• • •

CHAPTER IV

Training The Master

I embarked on the journey of training my Master, armed with the techniques and knowledge I had gathered from the book. The training process proved to be a challenging task, as teaching the commands required precision and consistency. According to the book, dogs have the capacity to remember up to 200 words, but the key was to keep the commands crisp and concise. Long, elaborate sentences would only confuse Master, so I had to stick to single words that he could easily grasp. It was a matter of saying the word and expecting Master to obey.

Until now, our walks had been more of a one-sided affair, with me being the one attached to Master rather than the other way around. But now, I wanted to establish a stronger bond and teach him the fundamental command of "Come." It was the simplest command to start with, and I decided to practice it at the nearby park. As an added incentive, I tucked some biscuits into my pocket, secretly planning to reward Master for his obedience. This time, I bought something for someone else rather than for myself.

I stood in the park, calling out to Master. He was too engrossed in his own exploration to respond to my voice. It seemed as though he didn't even recognize his own name. Disappointed but determined, I reached into my pocket and pulled out the biscuit packet. Ah, the power of the treat! It was like unleashing a magical spell that instantly captured Master's attention. I tried again, this time combining the command with the visual cue of the biscuit.

With renewed confidence, "Master, come! Come!" I repeated, waving the biscuit in the air. In that moment, a flicker of recognition sparked in Master's eyes. The tantalizing sight of the biscuit, combined with the command, seemed to awaken a dormant memory within him, as if he was conspiring to decode the message I was conveying. With a hop, skip, and a wagging tail, he made its way towards the tempting treat. Who needs four legs when you've got such zest and determination? It was like witnessing a furry superhero in action!

I understood that repetition and consistent training were essential for dogs to grasp commands fully. I would need to practice this exercise repeatedly, associating the command with the treat until Master responded to my call without the need for a bribe.

I diligently followed the training method outlined in the book, committed to helping Master understand the command "Master, come!" The biscuit became a vital tool in our journey, a visual cue that bridged the gap between words and actions. Time and time again, I called out to Master, making sure the biscuit was prominently displayed. Each repetition reinforces the link between the command and the desired response. I knew that slow and steady progress would eventually yield the results we both sought. Gradually, Master began to grasp the meaning behind my call. He realized that when I said those words, it was an invitation for him to come to me, to revel in the warmth of our bond.

Every correct response from Master was met with an outpouring of affection. I showered him with gentle pats on the head, praising him for his obedience and showering him with love. It was in those moments that I discovered the power of positive reinforcement.

• • •

The following day, armed with enthusiasm, Master and I ventured back into the park along with Fatso. Fatso, eager to witness the wonders of dog training firsthand, had joined our expedition. Earlier that morning at school, I had revealed Fatso with tales of my triumphs in teaching Master to "Come." I wondered if his excitement stemmed from a genuine interest in witnessing canine genius or simply the prospect of getting his paws on some biscuits.

Once we arrived at the park, I let Master play around for a while, enjoying the freedom of running and being untethered.

"So, bro, what's our training mission for this awesome dog?" Fatso asked, clearly impressed.

I smiled and replied, "Well, even perfect pups can learn new tricks! Master isn't meant to just eat and sleep all his life. He has plenty of things to learn."

Fatso nodded excitedly, fully on board with the plan. "Haha, okay! I don't want your biscuits if that's what you were referring to. We'll show off Master's skills and impress everyone in the park!"

"Right now, I want to teach him to come, sit, shake hands, and fetch. Later on, we can move on to more advanced commands like identifying a person or searching for a hidden object," I explained.

"Wow! Do you mind if I join you whenever you're training? It sounds like fun." Fatso requested.

"Sure, but only if you're not asking for biscuits," I joked.

I placed Master in front of me and noticed he was a bit restless. I wanted him to focus for a little while, so I tapped his head gently and said, "Master, relax."

"You're going to get biscuits if you give us a handshake, you know," Fatso tempted Master.

"You should avoid training the dog solely through food rewards because then it becomes dependent on them. Just a little praise and affection are more than enough to gain their confidence," I explained.

"Wow! Is that so? How do you know all this?" Fatso asked.

"I can read dogs' minds, you know," I lied playfully. "Now, shake hands," I said, lifting Master's paw into my palm.

"Thank you," she said as I congratulated by shaking her hand.

"That was a wonderful debate," I complimented her. The topic of debate centered around the choice between playing to win or finding enjoyment in the game itself. Our school often organized debate competitions to cultivate our speaking abilities and encourage imaginative thinking. Split into two teams, Ganga and Yamuna, I was with her on Team Ganga.

"You spoke really well. With you on our team, we have no worries about winning the champions' trophy," I said with elation.

"Thank you, but everyone else has contributed too. It's a team effort," she humbly replied. Debates were held every month, with points allocated based on each team's performance. At the end of the year, the team with the highest score would claim the coveted trophy. We held a substantial lead over Team Yamuna, largely due to the exceptional abilities of this remarkable girl. She possessed a unique talent for perceiving the beauty of things even with her eyes closed, and her heartfelt expressions eloquently conveyed this gift.

"It's my treat today. Let's go to the canteen," I suggested.

"Oh, sure. I'm ready," she smiled.

As we munched on our sandwiches, I asked her, "Where does happiness reside? In winning or in losing? Because I see people getting depressed after a loss, but I also see others becoming more motivated."

"Another debate session, huh?" she chuckled.

I used to shy away from participating in such debates because I never knew what to say. I was good at spinning yarns and telling lies, but unfortunately, those skills didn't serve me well in debates.

"If you want it to be," I replied.

"If they say that money brings happiness, then why does spending or giving it away also bring joy? If finding love brings delight, then why does sacrificing it bring peace? If one feels exuberant when praised by the world, then why does solitude bring joy? Happiness is everywhere, in gaining and losing alike. You just have to choose your path," she explained.

Nonetheless, my confusion persisted, leaving me in a state of silence. Sensing my uncertainty, she offered reassurance, "Don't worry! Someday, it will all become clear to you, and when that day arrives, I will extend my hand in a handshake of understanding." A gentle smile graced her lips.

With Master's paw in my hands, a sense of gratitude overwhelmed me. "Thank you," escaped my lips, instinctively acknowledging the depth of understanding that had blossomed within me. Now, I comprehended the essence of her words on that day. Nurturing my Master, ensuring his vaccinations, nourishment, and other necessities, I came to realize that the money I spent was not solely for my own benefit. Instead, it was invested in his well-being. Despite having received money from my mother to spend on myself, I consciously chose to save it, using those funds towards my Master's needs. Her wise words resonated in my mind, reminding me of the profound impact of selfless choices.

As I observed Master and Fatso playing together, I noticed how they had grown fond of each other's company. Fatso had become a close companion to Master, and it warmed my heart to see them bond. In this newfound understanding, I no longer feared choosing my own path. I realized that happiness could be found everywhere, both in gaining and in losing. All I had to do was search for my own path.

• • •

David's murder remained an unsolved mystery, and the search for his sister Elena's boyfriend continued. Despite lacking concrete evidence, my suspicion towards the bungalow man grew stronger. There was an inexplicable feeling within me that he might be responsible for this heinous act. I felt a personal responsibility to uncover the truth, but I wondered how I could accomplish this with only my loyal companion, Master, by my side.

I couldn't shake off the recollection of the old man lingering near the school premises in the days preceding David's untimely death. A chilling suspicion crept into my thoughts, hinting at the possibility that he might have been stalking Elena, David's sister. The notion took hold: had he cunningly ascertained their parents' absence, leaving the vulnerable siblings defenseless and isolated? This led me to theorize that the old man was responsible for the brutal attack that claimed David's life and caused Elena's mysterious disappearance. The pieces seemed to fit, yet my theory remained devoid of any concrete evidence, leaving it suspended in the realm of plausibility.

The question of how to prove my theory without evidence weighed heavily on my mind. It seemed like an insurmountable task. However, I was determined to find a way.

• • •

It has been a month since I started training Master, and I'm amazed at how quickly he has learned. Despite the missing leg, he hasn't encountered any other issues during the training process. Master has shown remarkable progress, exceeding my expectations. I have focused on establishing a solid foundation of basic commands, obedience, and good behavior.

"Won't the missing leg cause pain and stress for Master?" Fatso expressed his concern.

"I don't think so, Fatso," I reassured him. "Master has adapted well to his condition, and he doesn't seem to experience any discomfort or stress due to his missing leg. Dogs are incredibly resilient and can adjust to physical challenges."

Curiosity sparked in Fatso's eyes as he asked, "What's up for today's training?"

"I have covered a lot of basic commands and discipline training with Master, and he has made impressive progress," I replied. "Now, I want to focus on his instinctive and behavioral habits. And for a change, I thought we could play hide and seek."

Fatso's eyebrows shot up in surprise. "Hide and seek with a dog? Are you kidding, Rahul?"

"No, I'm serious. Do you know how dogs identify thieves and victims?" I asked Fatso.

"I only know that they can smell," Fatso replied.

"That's correct. Every person on this earth has a unique scent, just like unique DNA," I explained. "The odor of my sweat is not the same as yours. That's why dogs instinctively sniff anybody they meet for the first time. Did you know that a dog's sense of smell is 1,000 to 10,000,000 times greater than that of humans?"

"Wow, that's incredible," Fatso exclaimed, clearly fascinated by the information.

"Yeah, for now, remove your socks," I instructed Fatso, and he complied without questioning. "Just run and hide in a place where Master can't see you. I'll give you five minutes," I said, setting the rules for our game.

Fatso eagerly ran off with his bare feet to find a hiding spot. He was always enthusiastic when it came to trying out new training methods and engaging in activities with Master. We had chosen the empty space behind the old bungalow as our playground for this game of hide and seek. It provided enough room for hiding and added a sense of mystery to the whole experience.

After five minutes had passed, I called Master over and made him sniff Fatso's socks. Fatso had found a hiding spot in a small, dilapidated hut with a thatched roof, nestled under a massive peepal tree. As per the rules of the game, Fatso was supposed to sit and wait there until Master found him. However, his impatience got the better of him, and he started digging the sand and doodling to pass the time.

'Kiran <3 Pooja' he wrote on the sand, using a stick as a makeshift pen. As he continued darkening the inscription, he noticed a white, hard substance emerging from the sand. Fear crept over him, causing his heart to pound in his chest. Curiosity compelled him to clear away the mud around it, gradually revealing its true form. What he discovered left him in a state of shock and wonder.

"Fatso, are you here?" I called out, breaking his trance. Master had successfully found him. However, it was evident that something was amiss.

"What happened?" I asked, observing Fatso's awestruck expression. He remained silent for a moment, his finger trembling as he pointed towards the object he had uncovered. Intrigued, I quickly made my way to his side, joining him in the continued excavation to reveal the true nature of the discovery. With each passing moment, our anticipation grew. Finally, we unearthed a bone, bearing a resemblance to that of an animal, although we couldn't be certain. The fact that we were in the secluded area behind the bungalow, coupled with the strange actions of the old man, left us with a nagging sense that something peculiar was afoot. It became clear to me that I needed to unravel this mystery as soon as possible.

• • •

After numerous attempts to catch a butterfly, I finally succeeded. She had requested it, and I knew she wouldn't ask without a reason. I had my own motive for wanting to meet her, so I made my way to the orphanage.

"Here you go," I said as I handed her the bottle containing the captured butterfly, making sure there were holes at the top to allow for proper airflow.

"Oh, wow! You actually did it?" she exclaimed, clearly impressed.

"Yeah. Remember our deal? You promised to tell me a story if I managed to catch one," I reminded her, eager to hear what she had in store.

"Of course, I remember. But I thought you might have forgotten about it," she replied.

"I came all the way here for it. Are you free now?" I asked, my gaze fixed on the children who were deeply engaged in listening to her comforting words. Their innocence and resilience touched my heart, reminding me of the struggles they

faced without the presence of parents.

"Sure. Please have a seat on that bench under the tree. I'll join you in a minute," she replied, her voice carrying a sense of warmth and understanding.

As I settled onto the bench, a wave of emotions washed over me. The sight of these children, bearing the weight of the world on their small shoulders, stirred a mix of admiration, empathy, and compassion within me. They were facing challenges far beyond their years, yet their smiles and laughter echoed through the air, as if to defy the hardships they had endured.

Lost in contemplation, I found solace in the tranquil surroundings of the orphanage. The laughter and camaraderie among the children seemed to drown out the noise of the outside world, reminding me of the resilience of the human spirit in the face of adversity. It was in this moment, immersed in the presence of these incredible children, that she returned and took a seat beside me.

"You seem lost," she remarked, her voice filled with genuine concern, as if she could sense the whirlwind of emotions that had consumed me.

"Hmmm. I thought I had the greatest difficulties that nobody else could understand, but looking at these kids..." I trailed off, my words fading away, unable to express the depth of emotions surging within me. However, my thoughts were interrupted by a boy who caught my attention. Despite his physical challenges—having no legs and only one hand—he exuded an air of determination and purpose. He was engrossed in writing, his pen gliding across the paper.

"Is he doing his homework?" I inquired, curious about the boy's dedicated focus.

"No, he's writing. Most of the time, you'll find him engrossed in his writings. He aspires to be a writer," she responded, her gaze fixed on the boy with admiration. As I

observed him, a wave of humility washed over me, rendering me momentarily speechless.

In that moment, the boy's unwavering dedication and his unwritten stories spoke volumes. Despite his physical limitations, he possessed a boundless spirit and an indomitable will to pursue his passion.

"He lost his parents, his legs, and a hand in a terrible accident when he was a kid," she revealed softly, her voice filled with a mix of sadness and admiration.

"Oh! Please, don't share his story," I pleaded, my heart aching at the mere thought of the tragedy he had endured. "I'm not resilient enough to bear such sorrow. Can I, at least, read what he has written? Would that be alright?"

"Sure, why not?" she responded, leading me closer to the boy. He remained completely engrossed in his writing, unaware of our presence. I watched him intently, silently absorbing his determination and perseverance. Eventually, he finished his task, and sensing my curiosity, I mustered the courage to approach him.

"Excuse me," I spoke softly, "I noticed you've been writing, and I was wondering if I could read what you've written?"

He paused for a moment, his gaze penetrating into mine. Then, with a solemn expression, he handed me the paper

"Knowing things and experiencing them are different in the whole world," he murmured quietly before leaving without another word. I stood there, bewildered by his enigmatic statement, trying to comprehend its true meaning.

Returning to the bench where we had been seated, I unfolded the paper, eager to unravel the thoughts and emotions he had captured within his writing.

"I can't see," cried a blind man,

As I can't see the world.

An unknown voice within him replied,

"Cry not, my child, for you can still dream wide."
"I can't walk," cried the handicapped soul,
As I can't run or jump like everyone else.
The unknown voice in him consoled,
"Worry not, my son, for you can still make life's journey"
"I am deaf and dumb," cried a boy in despair,
As I can't share my thoughts through words.
The unknown voice in him comforted,
"Weep not, my boy, you can still express your feelings"
If you cannot find happiness with what you have,
you will never be happier even if you obtain all that you desire.

"Wow! I am speechless," I exclaimed.

"If you take a closer look, you'll find immense beauty in things that have been damaged, Rahul," she replied.

"By the way, what did he mean by 'the voice'?" I inquired.

"Someday, you will hear it," she smiled.

As we continued our conversation, a girl approached us. I was taken aback as she bore a striking resemblance to my girl. "Meet my friend Shwetha," she introduced her to me. They looked so alike, almost like twins, with matching height and complexion. The only difference was that Shwetha had her right leg missing, unlike my girl. They exchanged a few words in a hushed tone.

"Rahul, I have to go now. Can you please excuse us?" she requested.

"Sure," I replied, feeling a bit disappointed. "What about the butterfly story?" I asked.

"I promise I'll tell you tomorrow. Just bring me another butterfly," she said hurriedly, then rushed back inside. I watched them as they walked away. I couldn't fathom the kind of voice the boy had referred to, but I always heard my girl's voice echoing in my mind.

• • •

As usual, I was strolling with my Master near the serene riverside, a place that held a treasure trove of cherished memories for me. Gripping the leash, tied around Master's neck firmly, I walked along the familiar path. There was a constant fear within me, the fear that my master might suddenly dart away, pulling me along with him. Therefore, I made sure to hold onto the leash tightly, ensuring his safety and keeping us connected.

"Here, take your butterfly, my butterfly," I said, handing her the captured butterfly inside the bottle. Her face lit up with delight. We had made a pact to meet by the riverside, away from the bustling and inquisitive world of school.

"Enough with your mesmerizing exclamations," I teased, unable to contain my impatience any longer. "Tell me the story you promised. I can't wait any longer."

"Patience, my dear," she replied, a mischievous twinkle in her eyes. "I will tell you, just relax."

"I'm eagerly waiting," I exclaimed, a mixture of anticipation and impatience coursing through me.

We settled on our usual spot, a sturdy rock by the riverside, ready to indulge in the long-awaited story.

"Once upon a time, there was a girl who ventured into a magnificent garden. It was her first time in such a paradise. The sight of vibrant flowers, majestic trees, and the gentle rustling of leaves enchanted her. Amidst this symphony of beauty, a mesmerizing butterfly captured her attention. It fluttered gracefully from one flower to another, sipping nectar and spreading its colorful wings. The girl marvelled at the intricate patterns painted on the butterfly's delicate wings. How could something be so exquisitely adorned?" she began.

"As the girl continued to watch, a deep longing welled up inside her. She yearned to be like the butterfly, free to explore the world at will. Why did the butterfly possess such beauty and freedom that seemed elusive to her? Why was she bound and restricted, unable to pursue her passions? Why was she socially conditioned and unable to venture to fulfil her dream? These questions consumed her thoughts, haunting her every day," she continued, her voice carrying a sense of empathy for the little girl.

"In her quest to capture the happiness and colorful experiences she believed the butterfly possessed, the girl made a decision. She carefully caught the butterfly, imprisoning it within a bottle, envisioning a life filled with joy and vibrancy," she narrated, the anticipation building in the air.

She continued to gaze at the butterfly, but the joy and vibrancy she had seen before seemed to have vanished. It appeared dull and devoid of its previous enthusiasm. Overwhelmed with regret, she questioned herself, "What have I done? Why isn't it enjoying itself now?" She peered deep into the butterfly's eyes, searching for answers. After a moment of contemplation, she made a decision. Opening the cap of the bottle, she set the butterfly free once more. To her astonishment, she witnessed the happiness returning to the butterfly in an instant.

As the butterfly soared through the air, it felt a newfound sense of liberation. In its thoughts, it pondered, "Who is this girl who captured me but then released me? Many have tried to possess me, but this girl is different. She values my freedom above all else. Such a person is rare to find in this world." Drawn to the girl's unique spirit, the butterfly gracefully returned to her, alighting on her shoulders.

"That was truly a beautiful story," I remarked, appreciating the depth of its meaning.

"Thank you," she replied with a warm smile.

Curiosity aroused within me, and I couldn't help but ask, "Why did the butterfly return to her?"

She chuckled softly, recognizing my confusion. "Ah, my dear boy, that is something you will come to understand in due time," she replied cryptically, hinting at a deeper wisdom beyond my current grasp.

As I held Master by my side, I couldn't help but draw a parallel to the story. I had always clung tightly to him, fearing he might slip away. Yet, for a moment, I released my grip, allowing him the freedom to explore and roam. With a joyful limp, he ran and played all over the place, only to return to my side, standing still and content, wagging his tail in a beautiful display of acceptance.

In the gentle breeze, I heard her words echoing once again, "You will understand it someday, my boy."

• • •

"Fatso! We have to train our Master as soon as possible," I said.

"What's the hurry, Rahul? We have all the time in the world," Fatso replied lazily.

"Yeah, but I've given our Master a task. So, we both need to train him more seriously."

"By the way, do you have enough money to get him vaccinated next month? I've saved some money too." Fatso inquired.

"Yeah! I'm short on money, but I think we'll be able to manage within a month," I said.

"Hmmm."

"I read something new about a dog's capabilities yesterday. I thought I could share it with you so that it helps us train Master," I said.

"Oh, sure. I'm always ready," Fatso said, gulping two biscuits.

"The other day, we played hide and seek. Do you remember?" I asked, testing Fatso's memory.

"Yeah, I also remember the animal bone," Fatso said, laughing.

"Dogs have scenting ability, which means they can identify specific things or people using their olfactory powers. Even the laziest dogs have been known to pick up the scent of a female dog in heat from as far as two miles away, yet these same dogs show no interest in following other scents."

"Wow! To recognize a girl two miles away?!" Fatso was excited.

"The reason some dogs don't use their sense of smell is their lack of need. They don't have to track their prey since their food comes in a bag," I explained. For a moment, I pondered why Fatso didn't utilize his brain. Perhaps it was because he always found food wherever he went. At that moment, I understood he wasn't much different from any other dog.

"Go on, Rahul. Tell me more," Fatso urged me with enthusiasm.

"Most things that smell are organic, and getting warmer makes them smell stronger. This happens because heat breaks the smelly stuff into tiny pieces that float in the air. There are two main types of smells: the ones that stick to the ground and those that float in the air. Smells that float in the air, like body odor, come off animals and get carried by wind. Everyone has their own unique body smell, and it's strongest near where they are. As the smell travels farther, it gets fainter. These smells are really important clues that animals and even people leave behind when they move around."

"Are you saying that we're leaving a scent on the ground as we walk right now?" Fatso questioned.

"Yes, that's called track scent. A moving animal leaves its track scent, which becomes stronger as a tracking dog gets closer to the animal being tracked. In the case of humans, our body odor continuously sheds from our bodies, falls, and combines with the scent of our shoes and clothing. Some of this scent gets stamped into the soil, mixing with the odor of trampled ground cover. This ground cover consists of broken grass, twigs, and leaves that lie in the indentations on the surface of the soil. This combination of scents becomes a person's track scent."

"So, a criminal leaves clues wherever they go," Fatso replied, seemingly utilizing his brain for the first time in his life.

"Cold ground tends to retain scents, while warmer ground causes the scents to rise and disperse more quickly. A snow-covered track is easier to follow than one laid on warm ground," I continued.

"Very interesting," Fatso remarked.

"Can you guess how long a scent can remain on the ground?" I asked.

"I don't know, maybe a few minutes?" Fatso guessed.

"Track scents can persist for hours, or even several days, when the weather is foggy, misty, and windless. Under those conditions, the scent slowly rises from the track and remains a few inches above the ground. However, hot weather and dry wind can quickly disperse track scent," I explained.

"Bro, it's quite amazing. We have a lot of assignments to complete today. Weren't you aware of it? We can discuss this further tomorrow. Damn those trigonometry problems take up so much time!" Fatso exclaimed.

"Haha, since when did you start doing assignments, Fatso?" I teased him, bidding farewell for the day.

• • •

I made my way to school, knowing that for the first time in what felt like ages, I had completed all my assignments. Today, I wouldn't have to hang my head in shame. It's funny how we cherish the days when we've accomplished our tasks, but as we look back years later, we find ourselves reminiscing about the moments when we hadn't finished our work. The pain of the past often transforms into laughter in the future.

Entering the classroom with an abundance of energy, I was taken aback by the somber atmosphere. The class seemed unusually dull, and tension hung in the air.

"Hi, Arvind! What's up, buddy?" I greeted enthusiastically.

"Hi," Arvind responded, his voice low and devoid of its usual liveliness.

"What's wrong? Why is everyone so downcast?" I inquired, noticing that Arvind, Fatso, and Gopesh were engaged in a serious discussion.

"What's the matter, guys?" I pressed them further.

"Pooja has been missing since yesterday," Gopesh replied with a heavy sigh.

"Oh! Really? Perhaps she went to her friend's house," I suggested optimistically.

"We searched everywhere, but there's no trace of her. Her parents have even filed a police complaint," Gopesh informed me, his expression filled with worry. Fatso, in particular, appeared deeply disappointed. He had developed a fondness for Pooja.

"When was the last time anyone saw her?" I probed, concerned.

"I was with her on the way back home, but she went towards her house afterwards," Fatso replied, his voice tinged with sadness.

Her house was located on the opposite street, a short distance behind the eerie man's bungalow.

• • •

CHAPTER V

M For Murder

Fatso arrived at my house that evening, appearing visibly upset. He pulled out a gift-wrapped box from his bag and handed it to me.

"She gave this to me yesterday, bro," Fatso said, his voice filled with a mix of sadness and anticipation.

"Then why haven't you opened it yet?" I asked, curious.

"I wanted to open it in private, but my relatives unexpectedly visited our house yesterday, so I never got the chance," Fatso explained.

"Let me take a look," I said, taking the box from his hand. It felt surprisingly light, and a pang of concern crossed my mind. I hoped it wasn't something valuable like a gold ring.

Fatso snatched the box back, eager to unpack it as if he hoped to find her presence inside.

"Wait, Fatso! Don't open it," I interjected, a sense of urgency in my voice.

"Why not? We might find some clues. Don't you think so?" Fatso replied, his impatience apparent.

"No, Fatso. You could unintentionally destroy potential evidence. Just wait a moment," I said, rushing to my cupboard and retrieving a pair of gloves. Taking back the gift from Fatso, I carefully opened it while wearing the gloves, aware of the importance of preserving any possible clues.

"Open it quickly, bro," Fatso urged, his anxiety palpable.

As I peeled back the wrapping, a wave of relief washed over me when I saw a simple handkerchief inside. I didn't care about it, as long as it wasn't an expensive gift that Fatso would never share with me.

"Take a good look, Fatso," I said, unfolding the handkerchief. However, as we unravelled it completely, we discovered something cryptic stitched on it.

"What does it say, bro?" Fatso asked, squinting at the writing. "I can't make it out."

Taking the handkerchief back from him, I deciphered the cryptic letters: "P o o j a." The stitches were intriguing and attractive.

"Wow! It's so beautiful, isn't it?" Fatso exclaimed, captivated by the inscription.

"It's your gift. She should have stitched your name, not hers," I teased playfully. However, the gravity of the situation halted my jesting. I clung to the hope that Pooja had merely gone somewhere and would soon return.

With gloves on, Fatso snatched the handkerchief, to see her name embroidered on it. As he was looking at it, I realized there was more to the message. From the same word, when read in reverse, I could discern the letters "K i r a n." It was an ambigram—a word that could be read both right-side up as "Kiran" and upside down as "Pooja."

For a brief moment, I was stunned by the discovery. The ambigram held a deeper significance, sparking a surge of questions and uncertainties.

"Fatso, come on! Let's go find our master," I exclaimed, rushing out of my house towards the bungalow.

"What are you planning to do now, bro?" Fatso asked, trying to keep up with my pace.

"Didn't you see the gift? It's clear that she has feelings for you," I replied, my detective spirit kicking in.

"So what?" Fatso questioned, not fully grasping the significance.

"So, she must have painstakingly stitched that ambigram. It's a time-consuming task, and her sweat might be captured on the handkerchief. Now it's our master's job to take it from here and find Pooja," I explained, my mind racing with possibilities.

We brought our master to the spot where Fatso had last seen Pooja. I handed the handkerchief to our master, urging him to sniff it. Without hesitation, our master took off, and we followed closely behind. Fatso's excitement soared, and I could almost see the glimmer of hope in his eyes, as if he was already planning to propose to Pooja once we found her.

Our master led us on a determined sprint, and after about 15 minutes of intense running, he abruptly came to a stop in the backyard of the bungalow. It was the same place where Fatso had hidden during our recent game of hide and seek. Our master sniffed around the old hut, his senses finely attuned to any lingering scent. The suspense thickened as we held our breath, awaiting the next clue that could unravel the mystery of Pooja's disappearance.

Master continued to sniff the muddy ground inside the old hut, his instincts leading us to an unsettling discovery. Fatso stood frozen, unable to comprehend the intensity of the situation unfolding before us. The soil in that specific spot seemed unusually elevated, as if someone had recently disturbed it. My mind raced with a mix of anticipation and trepidation.

With a surge of determination, I hurried back to my house, retrieving a spade to unearth the hidden secret lurking beneath the surface. Every thud of the spade against the soil echoed with suspense, as I dug deeper, my heart pounding in my chest. Fatso, overwhelmed by the intensity of the moment, perspired profusely, his body trembling with nervous energy.

As the hole grew larger, my spade collided with an object, the clang reverberating through the air. I could feel it in my gut; this was no ordinary discovery. With bated breath, we cleared away the mud, unveiling the truth that sent a chill down our spines. It was a bone—a bone that should not have been there.

Realizing the urgency of the situation, we wasted no time. We swiftly contacted the authorities, summoning the police to the scene.

• • •

"Sir, the post-mortem report indicates that the body we found is Elena's, David's elder sister" Constable Kannan reported.

"So, someone must have killed her a month ago and buried the body," Suresh responded.

"Sir, there are signs of a rape attempt on Elena as well."

"This appears to be the work of a psychopath. Have you discovered any leads regarding Pooja?"

"Not yet, sir."

"I have questioned Kiran, who claims to be her boyfriend, but the information is unclear and inconclusive."

• • •

After a week, Fatso returned to school, seemingly recovered from the shock. The class felt strangely dull, and I couldn't help but miss both Fatso and Arvind, who had been absent due to health issues. How things had changed! I found myself wondering anxiously about what the future held for us.

"Hey, Fatso. How are you holding up?" I cautiously inquired.

"I'm... okay, bro," Fatso replied hesitantly.

"I really missed you, man." I confessed, unsure of how he would react.

The police had questioned Fatso extensively, suspecting him as Pooja's lover. Yet, somehow, they didn't seem to find any evidence to support their suspicions. It was hard to believe that Fatso could be capable of such a crime.

"Yeah, bro. This week has been a nightmare. Somehow, I managed to get through it. But I'm extremely worried about Pooja. Who knows where she is or how she's doing?!" Fatso's voice wavered with concern.

The police had interviewed everyone in our class, gathering statements from each student. Surprisingly, no one seemed to be under suspicion.

"I'm relieved that you're back, Fatso. Even Arvind is sick and admitted in hospital for a week" I said, embracing him tentatively.

"Rahul, there's been a question lingering in my mind since last week," Fatso began uncertainly.

"What is it?" I asked, bracing myself for the unknown.

"How did Master discover Elena's body? We made him smell Pooja's handkerchief, right? But how is that even possible? Maybe Master couldn't recognize Pooja's scent," Fatso proposed, his tone filled with doubt.

"No, Fatso. Master was right. He wouldn't be able to find Elena if we gave him Pooja's scent," I replied, my own confidence faltering.

"Then... how did it happen?" Fatso's voice trailed off, confusion evident in his words.

"Perhaps... maybe it wasn't Pooja who embroidered the ambigram on the handkerchief. Maybe it was Elena all along. Pooja might have waited until she felt emotionally prepared to reveal it to you," I suggested, my uncertainty mirroring his own.

"I don't fully grasp it, bro. I need some time to process everything," Fatso admitted, his voice tinged with a mix of bewilderment and contemplation.

● ● ●

Amidst all this confusion, I longed for the presence of my girl. She had a way of guiding me towards the right path. With midterm exams approaching next week, everyone seemed to be immersed in their studies. It was a positive distraction, allowing us to divert our minds to something productive. When our hearts are vulnerable, it's often beneficial to engage our minds in meaningful tasks.

I mustered up the courage to ask my mom if I could bring my master to our house. However, she flatly refused. I used to secretly feed master every day, sneaking food from my kitchen. I truly missed him, but with my exams looming, I eagerly awaited their completion so that I could once again play with Master, just like we always had.

After my exams, a strong sense of nostalgia washed over me. All I yearned for was to escape and lose myself in the memories of days gone by. Unfortunately, there seemed to be no destination that could recreate the magic of a particular place—a place that had held a special significance throughout my entire life.

It was the riverside, a sanctuary I frequented week after week. The river itself was a tale, an epic narrative unfolding with every passing moment. It flowed relentlessly, defying the constraints of time and circumstance. Storms, rain, scorching heat, bitter cold—none of it mattered to this majestic river. It simply continued its ceaseless journey, flowing and flowing until it finally merged with the vastness of the sea. Nearly four kilometers downstream, the river found its ultimate destination at the Bay of Bengal.

I couldn't help but reminisce about the time, nearly two years ago, when I had taken a stroll through the river's gentle currents, hand in hand with my beloved. The memory remained etched in my mind, a cherished moment that had united us with the vastness of the ocean.

"You know what? I got kicked out of the Under-17 school team yesterday. They didn't select me, claiming that I can't handle situations adequately. They also complained about my inability to handle pressure," I said, expressing my disappointment.

"Never mind, Rahul. You can always give it another try," she said, attempting to console me.

"I'm done with cricket. I'm going to switch to football. You know, in football, you can earn much more than in cricket, right?" I said, trying to convince her.

"What if the football team also rejects you for the same reasons?" she fired back.

"I don't know. But I can't continue playing cricket anymore. The board is plagued with dirty politics. The board members seem to play more games than the actual players. You have no idea how tough it is unless you've experienced it firsthand. My mind still yearns to play cricket, but my heart is too fragile to endure the constant rejection."

We remained silent for a few minutes. She didn't reply. It was just two of us, the river, and the beautiful small mountains surrounding us. After a while, she broke the silence.

"Do you see the mountains around us?" she asked politely.

"Of course. Why are you being cryptic when I'm feeling so frustrated?" I exclaimed.

"Are they beautiful?" she inquired.

Taking a moment to calm down, I replied, "Yes, they are."

"The mountains are beautiful precisely because of their ups and downs, aren't they?" she remarked.

I understood what she was trying to convey. She was consoling me, reminding me that experiencing disappointment and rejection is a common part of life.

"You don't know what's really happening in the team. My own teammates are trying to get me run-out. How can I play with them? It's just a dirty game out there. You don't understand, you don't understand," I yelled at her, tears welling up in my eyes.

"Look over there," she said, pointing towards the swamp beside the river. The swamp had separated itself from the river and was filled with dirt and weeds. Although a few lotus flowers bloomed, no one desired to venture down there.

"I wish I could regain my place in the team," I said.

"Yes! Life can be like a ditch, but you can be the lotus within it," she said, gesturing towards those lovely flowers that thrived even in stagnant water. That's why they are admired so much and also the national flower.

"I agree with you. I performed exceptionally well last season. I was among the top five batsmen, and it was almost certain that I would become the next captain of our team. I was elated. Everything seemed so promising and clear. But now, it's all an illusion," I said, my expression turning gloomy as I fought back tears.

"Do you see that you're not in control? You were happy when everything was going well, but now you're crying. Don't you think the board members were right?" she asked, surprising me with her directness instead of offering consolation.

"Isn't it natural for everyone to cry when they're sad and laugh when they're happy? What's wrong with being human? What do you think I should do?" I asked, my voice filled with emotion.

"When your heart is weak and despondent, listen to your mind. Listen to your heart when you're overflowing with joy and pride in your accomplishments. But right now, listen to your mind. Go out there, play, and find your place in the team again," she enlightened me.

"Yeah, I'll do as you say," I responded, determined to follow her advice.

"Good boy," she said, affectionately pinching my cheek.

"One last question," I asked.

"You always say that, but you never stop asking more questions," she laughed.

"Haha, there are people who constantly insist that I must do things their way. Yet, when I begin doing things in their suggested manner, they expect me to do it differently. And when I'm confused and don't do anything, they scold me. How can I convince such people?" I poured out my frustration to her.

"If it's sunny, they complain it's too hot. If it rains, they grumble about the slush. And if it's calm for a while, they lament the monotony of life. How can you ever make such people happy?" she replied.

"That's exactly what I was asking, and now you're throwing the same question back at me," I frowned at her.

She laughed. "I thought you understood what I meant, but never mind. Let's walk alongside the river until it reaches the ocean."

"It's four kilometers away. Can you walk that far?" I asked.

She didn't reply, but her silence spoke volumes. 'Okay, as you say. Anywhere and anything for you, my dear,' I thought to myself, ready to embark on the journey beside her.

After nearly two hours, with each step closer to the beach, the sound of crashing waves grew louder, hinting at the magnificent sight that awaited us.

And then, there it was—a breathtaking panorama that stretched as far as the eye could see. The ocean, adorned in shades of deep blue, sparkled under the warm rays of the sun. The waves rolled rhythmically, cresting and breaking in a mesmerizing dance. The salty breeze gently caressed our faces, carrying with it the unmistakable scent of the sea—a refreshing and invigorating aroma.

The horizon seemed endless, merging seamlessly with the sky in a captivating display of nature's grandeur. The vastness of the ocean invoked a sense of awe and wonder, as if witnessing a living entity with its own heartbeat. It felt as though time stood still in that moment, allowing us to immerse ourselves in the sheer magnificence of this natural wonder.

"The ocean stretches so far, yet it feels so close to us. It holds countless secrets within its depths, yet it remains so tranquil," she remarked, her eyes sparkling with delight, as if she had reunited with an old friend.

The aroma of freshly caught fish wafted through the air, tempting my taste buds. Fishermen had successfully reeled in a bountiful shoal of fish. Nearby, women skilfully fried the fish with their magical blend of spices, enticing passersby along the coastline.

"Shall we have some fish? My mouth is watering," I suggested, gazing longingly at the tantalizing aroma. However, she continued to gaze at the struggling fish, gasping for breath

and writhing in their final moments of life.

"Leaving the world, yet living for the world," she murmured, her eyes still fixed on the dying fish.

"Oh God! You must have devoured a giant book of philosophy as a baby. No more of it, please. I'm already drowning in your profound thoughts. I'm gasping for breath, and all I can smell is you," I playfully teased her.

Her laughter filled the air, a joyful melody that echoed against the backdrop of the ocean waves.

We sat on the sandy beach, indulging in the savory delight of the fried fish. Our gazes were fixed upon the enchanting sunset, as the sun slowly descended towards the horizon. It appeared as if the sun was sinking into the sea, seeking assistance, yet there was no one to offer aid. Despite its plight, the sun radiated its brilliance, illuminating the beach and sharing its beauty with all who were present.

Immersed in the captivating scenery, I turned to her and posed a question about my future. Lost in her own thoughts, she gestured towards the distant sun and responded, "Shine. Even from afar, your radiance will be admired."

Her responses were always filled with poetic wisdom, painting vivid imagery in my mind. As we strolled along the shoreline, our footsteps left imprints in the sand, I followed in her footsteps, placing my feet where she had walked. Ironically, she left only a single footprint, emphasizing the unfairness of life. Observing the relentless waves washing ashore, I contemplated how life can be so capricious, erasing all traces of our existence with each gentle sweep.

"You know what?" I said, breaking the silence.

"Tell me," she responded, her eyes fixated on the shoreline as she created a footprint in the salty sand, awaiting the embrace of the incoming waves.

"I remember what you said about following the heart when it's weak and listening to the mind when it's joyful," I began, a hint of uncertainty in my voice. "But what if there's a conflict between the two? What should I do then?"

A soft laughter escaped her lips as she turned to face me. "What prompted this question, Mr. No-more-philosophy?" she teased.

I chuckled, trying to hide my curiosity. "Just to know more, you know," I shrugged. "My mind wants to thrash that guy who caused my run-out, yet my heart longs to forgive and focus on the game."

"Follow your heart," she advised, her voice filled with tenderness.

I sighed, contemplating her words. "Hmm, thank you," I whispered gratefully.

"That's what Swami Vivekananda once said," she added. "'In a conflict between the heart and the brain, follow your heart.'"

"Oh, no wonder you delve into the wisdom of saints," I remarked playfully.

"Yes, I share it with the children at the orphanage every evening," she shared with a gentle smile.

"Would you mind sharing some of that wisdom with me as well?" I asked, my eyes filled with genuine curiosity.

"Of course, why not?" she replied, her warmth enveloping my heart.

"One last question," I said, knowing well that it wouldn't truly be the last. "Will you be with me in the future?" feeling a bit shy.

Her laughter filled the air, a sound that echoed with joy and affection. "I'm feeling quite tired. Could you carry me back?" she requested, her eyes sparkling.

"Absolutely," I answered, a surge of delight coursing through me.

And so, I held her in my arms, cherishing the closeness between us. She playfully pinched my cheeks, a sweet gesture that made my heart flutter, reminding me of the love we shared and the beautiful journey that lay ahead.

As I returned to the present reality, a sense of solitude engulfed me. There was no one to satisfy my curious queries anymore. The countless questions I had posed to her, sometimes foolish and sometimes profound, were now left unanswered. She had always responded with profound insights that stirred my very soul. The butterflies, the vibrant flowers, and the flowing river had been the silent witnesses to our exchanges, our stories, and our moments of contemplation. It dawned on me that just as a few flowers have the power to transform a desolate landscape, a few individuals have the ability to make life itself beautiful. Few flowers make the barren land beautiful but few people make life meaningful.

• • •

We had a week off after our exams, so I decided to resume training with my Master. It had been quite some time since our last session, and I hoped he hadn't lost his touch. As usual, Fatso joined me.

"Hey, Master. How have you been? It feels like ages since I last saw you," Fatso greeted Master while patting his head.

Master responded by showering Fatso with licks all over his face.

"Fatso, let's go for a walk," I suggested.

"Yeah, I can't wait to play with Master again. Have you found any clues about the perpetrator of those crimes? Pooja is still missing, and I'm losing hope," Fatso expressed his concern.

We began our walk, with Master leading the way, and my mind filled with a mixture of determination and worry. The training session was on my mind, but the unresolved mysteries of David and Pooja's disappearance weighed heavily on my heart.

"No, Fatso. After we discovered the body, I searched the buried place thoroughly, but I didn't find any significant clues. I did come across a few bone fragments, though," I explained.

"Rahul, remember when we were playing hide and seek with Master the other day, we found a bone too. Perhaps it was left there as a marker, like a flag," Fatso suggested.

I couldn't comprehend the reasoning behind such a peculiar method of leaving clues. It seemed illogical to intentionally lead oneself to be caught by the police. "No, Fatso. I don't see any logical explanation for that. I made Master sniff around the burial site, but it yielded no results. I'm at a loss for any substantial leads," I replied, frustration evident in my voice.

As we continued walking along the road, a garbage truck passed by, emitting a foul odor that made me grimace and cover my nose in disgust. "Ugh! That smell is horrendous," I muttered.

Fatso pondered aloud, "I wonder how the driver manages to tolerate that stench all the time. If I were in his place, I'd probably pass out. Master could easily identify criminals if they all smelled like that garbage."

Chuckling at Fatso's remark, I explained, "Well, Fatso, the driver can't smell the garbage because he's accustomed to it"

"Oh! How come? It is right behind him all the time,"

"It is because the human olfactory system is designed in such a way. This is because of our relatively small number of olfactory cells, and we also develop an immunity to certain smells over time. Humans become accustomed to odors quite quickly," I explained.

"I didn't quite understand, bro," Fatso looked puzzled.

"Let me give you a relatable example. Have you ever smelled the aroma of freshly baked chocolate cookies in a bakery? Well, the bakery workers are deprived of this heavenly experience. After the first day, they can't even detect the smell anymore," I explained vividly.

"Oh, I see," Fatso exclaimed, his understanding improving when the topic revolved around food.

"But dogs, on the other hand, don't seem to become accustomed to scents. Their sense of smell remains sharp in their memory, and even if a trail is repeatedly interrupted, they can still pick it up and follow it," I explained.

"Wow, maybe they are more intelligent than us," Fatso mused.

"No, Fatso. It's not about intelligence. Dogs might not reach the same level of abstract reasoning as humans, but certain breeds like the German Shepherd have exceptional memory capabilities. Once they grasp and store a particular activity in their memory, they rarely forget it," I clarified.

"That's a brilliant idea, Fatso. If we can bridge that gap with our reasoning, we can definitely use Master as bait to catch the culprit," I replied.

"Exactly!" Fatso agreed.

"So, what's your next plan? You mentioned wanting to make Master a cop," he asked.

"Yes, that's the plan. I want to get him a CGC test, and once he passes that, we can move forward with our mission," I explained.

"What's CCC bro", Fatso enquired

"Haha, no Fatso, it's not CCC, it's CGC - Canine Good Citizen test," I clarified, chuckling at his confusion. "The test is designed to assess a dog's behavior and obedience in public. It's not a competitive test, so there's no need to worry about winning or losing."

Fatso seemed relieved. "Oh, I like those non-competitive tests, bro! What kind of tasks do they evaluate during the test?"

"It's a series of simple tasks, Fatso," I explained. "For example, they assess how the dog interacts with a friendly stranger, how they walk through a crowd without getting anxious, how they respond to commands when called, how they handle distractions without reacting, their overall appearance and grooming, and their behavior around other dogs."

As we continued strolling down the streets, our conversation took us back to the memories of the past, knowing that in just six months' time, after our 12th grade exams, we would all embark on separate journeys to pursue our individual dreams. Suddenly, my attention was drawn to two street dogs at the far end of the road. These dogs were notorious for their incessant barking, often causing annoyance to the people in the vicinity. Hoping that Master wouldn't engage in a confrontation with them, I cautiously approached. As we neared the dogs, I noticed the familiar faces of my classmates, Arvind, Gopesh, and Nizam, riding their bicycles on their way to swimming class.

"Hey guys!" Gopesh's voice echoed through the street, breaking the silence. As if triggered by the commotion, my Master began barking vigorously, while the street dogs joined in, creating a cacophony of canine voices.

"Hello everyone! Arvind, it's great to see you up and about. I'm glad you've recovered," I called out, trying to maintain a conversation amidst the noisy chaos.

To regain control, I pulled Master's leash closer to me, preventing any further movement. He was clearly agitated, and the barking persisted, making it difficult for us to communicate properly.

"Guys, I think it's best if we move on. These dogs seem quite wild. Let's catch up tomorrow in school," Arvind suggested, realizing the need to disengage from the chaotic situation.

I quickly took control of Master, pulling him away from the street and distancing ourselves from the barking dogs. As we reached a different street, I noticed that Master had regained his composure, appearing calm and collected once again.

"Rahul. I am afraid Master might fail in his 'reaction to another dog' test. He was never so aggressive." Fatso said.

"Yeah, Fatso, I've never seen him like this either. Maybe I need to work on this and train him more," I replied, realizing the importance of addressing Master's aggressive behavior. We walked back towards my house, contemplating the best approach to provide the necessary training and support for Master.

• • •

The next day, we began our training early in the morning. "Fatso, did you know that a few of our classmates went trekking? They will be climbing mountains, and it sounds incredibly adventurous," I said.

"Oh, no, bro. I don't enjoy climbing. It's tiring and exhausting. Eventually, they all end up back where they started. So, what's the point of the whole endeavor?" Fatso fired back at me.

"You're one hell of a lazy guy who won't even do a tiny job to burn off your belly fat," I teased him.

"Whatever, bro. What are you going to teach Master today?" Despite his love for laziness, he was always active when it came to being with my Master and participating in his training.

"Fatso, I've been reading about dog shows. It's a place where we can compete with professional handlers for trophies. There will be many skilled people in the competition. It could be a great platform to showcase our Master's talents. I just hope that someone will recognize his abilities."

"Rahul, don't take this the wrong way, but I still don't believe that you can make Master a cop. Let's just have him with us, and we can play with him for the rest of our lives. Besides, the police already have their own trained dogs. Why would they choose Master over others?" Fatso's words hit me with disappointment. In a way, he was right. Master had a missing leg and no experienced handler. But deep down, I knew I was doing all of this without any reason, purely out of love.

"Fatso, no matter what, I'm going to do everything I can to make him a cop. But for now, let's focus on the training. Today, we'll teach him how to climb up and down the A-Frame." I said, setting aside my worries about the training's outcome.

"What is it? A-Frame?"

"An A-Frame is a structure used in dog training. Look here," I said, picking up two pieces of plywood. "A regulation A-Frame is constructed by hinging these two pieces of plywood in the center. Instead of setting it up with the peak several feet above the ground, I will lay it nearly flat on the ground with the center elevated only a few inches."

I encouraged Master to move back and forth across the A-Frame, helping him become familiar with the obstacle.

"And then?" Fatso asked, curious to know the next step.

"Then I would raise the hinge to a few meters above the ground level," I explained.

"It's like climbing a small mountain. It can be a fun challenge for Master." replied Fatso

Fatso seemed to be intrigued by the idea now, despite his earlier reluctance towards trekking. As Master struggled to climb the A-Frame, possibly due to his missing leg, Fatso encouraged him by patting gently.

"C'mon Master, you can do it!" Fatso cheered, and slowly, albeit at his own pace, Master managed to run over the A-Frame.

"Good job!" I shouted, feeling proud of Master's progress. Fatso jumped with joy and suggested, "Bro, let's go for trekking tomorrow!"

I chuckled at Fatso's sudden change of heart and replied, "Sure, why not? It'll be a great adventure for all of us."

• • •

CHAPTER VI

Nobody Is Orphan

I wanted to visit the orphanage; it had been a very long time since my last visit. As I approached the familiar building, I noticed how the walls were worn and weathered. There was nothing particularly appealing about the exterior, but deep inside, this place held a special meaning for me. Standing at the gate, I caught a glimpse of Shwetha walking along the corridor. If my beloved girl were still alive, she would resemble Shwetha.

"Hi Shwetha!" I called out, raising my voice to ensure she could hear me. She turned and made her way towards me, a warm smile on her face.

"Hi Rahul! How have you been? It's been such a long time," Shwetha greeted me, her voice filled with genuine joy.

"Yeah," I replied, a mixture of emotions welling up inside me.

"So, how are your studies going, Shwetha?" I asked, genuinely curious about her progress.

"Fine, Rahul," she replied with a hint of pride in her voice. "And how is everyone at school and your parents?"

In that moment, I realized how selfless these children were, always concerned about others regardless of their own circumstances. "Everyone is doing well, Shwetha. Thank you for asking. How about everyone here?" I inquired, stepping out of my comfort zone to express genuine interest in their lives.

"Yeah, sort of everyone is fine," she responded softly, her head slightly bowed.

I sensed that something was amiss, a lingering issue weighing on her mind. "Tell me, is there something wrong? I'm here to help you," I offered, hoping to provide support in any way I could.

"Oh, no, nothing like that," Shwetha reassured me, her voice tinged with resilience. "It's just the usual problems we face. We'll figure it out. We've experienced even worse."

While I acknowledged that their struggles far surpassed anything I had encountered, I couldn't help but feel compelled to assist them in whatever small way I could.

"Listen, Shwetha, I know that I'm just a kid who sometimes complains about petty problems. But please know that I'm here to help you in any way I can," I assured her sincerely.

She responded with a soft acknowledgment, and then began sharing their current predicament. "It's just that we're facing a severe financial crisis. We no longer have enough money to sustain the orphanage, and we've accumulated substantial debt. We're not receiving any donations, and there's no significant income. Meanwhile, the expenses keep piling up." "Mother", referring to Prathibha Bai, the elderly woman who dedicated herself to caring for these children, "is deeply worried and has fallen ill."

Deeply concerned, I asked, "How much money do you need, Shwetha?" Although I knew that my financial contributions would be limited, I wanted to understand the scale of their situation.

"Approximately sixteen to twenty lakhs, at least," she replied.

"Oh my God," I exclaimed, overwhelmed by the magnitude of the sum. "I've never even seen that much money in my life."

As if their financial struggles weren't enough, Shwetha continued, "Furthermore, this place is deteriorating rapidly. We need to either reconstruct it or find an alternative location."

Feeling a sense of helplessness, I apologized, saying, "I'm sorry that you're going through all of this. I wish there was more I could do."

"I am missing her too much. She was incredible at handling crises, and even though we may share a resemblance, I can never manage things the way she did."

Shwetha's words echoed my own thoughts, and I responded with a thoughtful, "Hmm... Don't worry, I will always be there for you."

As tears continued to flow, Shwetha sobbed, "If my father was alive, things would never be like this."

I recalled my girl sharing stories about Shwetha's profound love for her late father. Even though he had passed away when she was very young, Shwetha would speak of him every day and dream of being reunited with him. In that moment, I struggled to find the right words to comfort her. Instead, I remained by her side, allowing her to express her grief fully. I understood the weight of her loss and the longing she felt.

After shedding tears and pouring out her heart, Shwetha looked up at me and said, "Hey Rahul, I have something for you."

"Oh, really? What is it?" I asked, with curiosity. Despite the somber atmosphere, her smile managed to bring a glimmer of joy.

She disappeared into the room momentarily and returned, handing me a piece of paper. I took it, unsure of what to expect. In that moment, my mind wandered, briefly entertaining the possibility of a romantic gesture, but I quickly snapped back to reality. "Can I read it?" I asked, still feeling a bit confused.

"Sure! But let me first tell you the story behind this," she replied, her voice tinged with anticipation.

"Not again!" I thought to myself, feeling slightly exasperated. It seemed like girls always had stories to tell me. "Yeah, tell me," I replied, preparing myself for another tale.

"Two years ago, one day, I was crying, thinking about my father," she began. If women didn't know how to cry, maybe men wouldn't have listened to them. I thought to myself.

She continued, "It was then that she wrote a poem to console me. I was complaining that there was nobody to love me." A pang of self-consciousness hit me for a moment. Wasn't I here for her? No matter what difficulties or hardships she faced, the presence of a beautiful girl could momentarily make them disappear. That was the enchanting power these angels held.

"What did she write?" I enquired, unable to contain my interest.

"Go on, read it yourself," she said politely, handing me the paper.

"God appeared in a boy's dream,
Granted him a wish to meet him.
On a roadside, where he had lost his hand,
But warned, not to be late even for a second.
Overjoyed by his appearance,
The boy left home filled with exuberance.
The day he was waiting for,
Hoping to gain what he lost afar.
On his path, he saw a blind lady who had lost her way,

The boy wished to help but he would be late, so he gave it away.

After taking a few steps, feeling his heart cry,

Never had he abandoned anyone who needed him to standby.

Alas, he turned back, helping her with his only hand,

The boy knew he would be late, but took his stand.

Happiness is not about gaining his hand, but not failing to understand

Choosing between the one who loves you and the one who needs love.

In the former, you live. In the latter, there is life."

It felt like a déjà vu. I recalled experiencing a similar situation in front of our school. One day, I was running late for cricket training when I noticed a blind lady attempting to cross the road. Caught up in my hurry, I didn't bother to assist her and hurried past. However, after taking a few steps, a pang of guilt and empathy surged within me. I couldn't shake off the feeling of wanting to help her. So, I turned back and approached the elderly lady, offering my assistance to safely navigate the road. Perhaps my girl had been silently watching me at that moment. However, in the poem, she portrayed breaking one of my hands. If she were here now, I would have proven to her the strength of my arms with a punch.

Interrupting my thoughts, Shwetha asked, "What are you thinking, Rahul?"

With a quick recovery, I replied, "Oh, nothing! I was just admiring her," attempting to conceal the mixed emotions and memories that flooded my mind.

"Yeah! She had said that you are the inspiration for the poem. I wanted you to keep it"

I nodded with a silent gesture of acceptance.

• • •

Gopesh had invited all our friends to his house, not for any particular occasion, but just to hang out and spend time together. He had planned for us to watch a movie. When I arrived at 11 in the morning, Gopesh, Fatso, Arvind, and Nizam were engrossed in conversation.

"Hey guys!" I greeted them.

"Hey Rahul, what's up, dude?" Arvind welcomed me.

"Did your doggy finally stop barking?" Nizam taunted me. He could be quite rude at times, and I wasn't fond of him.

"If I had let him loose that day, he would have bitten off the thing you value the most," I retorted, not backing down.

"So your doggy runs around biting other nuts, huh?" Nizam continued to provoke me.

"Enough with the arguing, guys!" Gopesh intervened, trying to bring some peace.

"Now, what's the plan?" Arvind raised his voice to redirect the conversation.

"How about making chapatis?" Nizam attempted to mock Arvind.

"That's not funny, Nizam," Arvind sarcastically replied.

"Guys, please, let's have some fun. How about watching a movie? I have a great collection - Tom Cruise, Sylvester Stallone, Bruce Willis. You name it," suggested Gopesh.

"Do you have a movie that I care about the most?" Nizam asked with an evil smile. Everyone understood what kind of movie he was referring to. All ears were focused, with more concentration than during our classes. Fatso's jaw dropped, and his mind was already preparing for it. And I knew everybody would agree to it.

"I'm sorry, guys. My granny is upstairs. What if she comes down suddenly?" Gopesh said.

"Never mind, Gopesh. I'll change the channel as soon as she comes," Arvind suggested.

Everyone smiled at each other, trying to maintain the positive atmosphere. As we continued discussing, Gopesh's granny came downstairs and sat in the corner, engrossed in mending her clothes.

"Oh no... she has come down," Gopesh grumbled softly. Our hopes were shattered instantly. The excitement we had felt had now evaporated, disappearing like the morning dew under the scorching sun.

"Hmm, guys, I have an awesome thriller movie. Let's watch it now, and once my granny goes upstairs, we can switch to what's on everybody's mind," Gopesh suggested. It was a brilliant idea to keep the fantasy going.

"He's right, guys," Arvind agreed.

Gopesh started playing the movie, and everyone became engrossed in it. The movie revolved around a murderer and a police officer's investigation. In one scene, a man attempted to rape a girl and brutally killed her, dragging her lifeless body out of the house and burying her in the backyard.

We all felt a sense of unease, as a similar incident had occurred a couple of months ago on our street. Fatso had particularly been affected by it. It was like reliving the terrifying events on the screen. While the lead actor might solve the case within two hours in the movie, Elena's killer was still out there, with no clues whatsoever.

As we continued watching, Fatso became increasingly uncomfortable. He abruptly got up and headed to the kitchen to fetch some water.

"I can't watch it, guys. You all carry on. I'll go outside," Fatso said, his voice filled with unease. The movie was paused, freezing the scene where the man had just buried the girl with a spade in his hands.

"Come on, Kiran. It's just a movie. Don't be scared," Gopesh tried to reassure him. But Fatso's distress was evident.

"Let him go and get some fresh air, Gopesh," I interjected. I understood that Fatso needed a break from the intense atmosphere.

"He seems really disturbed. I'll go with him. You guys continue watching," Arvind offered, sensing Fatso's discomfort.

"Come on, Arvind. Fatso's just nervous. He'll be fine. Besides, what if grandma goes upstairs?" Nizam winked mischievously. His comment sparked laughter among everyone, momentarily lightening the tension in the room.

"I'll be back in a few minutes. You guys carry on," Arvind pleaded and left the room, following Fatso.

The movie resumed, and everyone remained engrossed in the story until the end. I hoped that I might find some clue or inspiration from the movie to help solve the real-life mystery. However, the harsh reality was different. Arvind and Fatso had missed the suspense and thrills of the story unfolding on the screen. My concerns were consumed by the fact that the actual murderer was still at large, and we remained clueless about their identity.

• • •

The next day, I resumed my training routine, and Fatso joined me once again. Concerned for his well-being, I asked, "Are you okay, Fatso?"

"Yeah, bro. It was haunting me. I can't stop thinking about Pooja. Will they ever find out what happened to her? Will they catch Elena's murderer?" He sighed, his mind burdened with unanswered questions.

"I wish I had the answers, Fatso. But don't worry, we will find a way," I reassured him.

"How?" he asked, his voice filled with uncertainty.

"I don't know yet," I admitted honestly.

"Hmm," he replied, contemplating our next move.

"Let's teach our master something aggressive. I didn't want to resort to this, but we don't have much choice," I proposed.

"What do you mean, bro?"

"Schutzhund training," I said decisively.

"Huh?? Sh..SH..shu what?" Fatso replied. It was definitely a tongue twister for him. He didn't have the slightest hint of the word."

"Schutzhund means 'protection dog' in German. And yes, Schutzhund is primarily a sport for dogs, but it's more than just a game. It tests the dog's skills, intelligence, and ability to perform tasks related to protection, tracking, and obedience. It's a way to train and assess the capabilities of working dogs like German Shepherds."

"Oh! Is it a sport for dogs? But I can't pronounce it bro. Sh Shu sh." Fatso struggled.

"For your sake we shall call it 'bow bow' training." I convinced him. It is easier to train hundred dogs than to teach pronunciation to Fatso.

"Hahaha" He laughed.

"Imagine a competition for dogs where they show off their skills just like athletes! This competition, called Schutzhund, helps see which dogs of any breed are best suited for important jobs like helping police. Dogs that do well in Schutzhund are good at many things, not just police work. They can also sniff out special smells, find people who are lost, and even help in emergencies. In this competition, dogs show off their skills in three main ways: finding smells, following commands perfectly, and protecting their handler. So, if a dog shines in Schutzhund, it's a good sign they can be a superhero dog in many different ways!" I explained to Fatso like a kid.

"Bro!" Fatso interrupted.

"Do you want me to continue or not?" I was a little irritated.

"Ya I want to know more. But please use our code word 'Bow-bow' and not 'Shshhsh'." Fatso struggled to pronounce.

"Okay! Bow bow has three phases, tracking, obedience and protection." I started.

"I think Master already knows how to track scents," Fatso replied.

"Yeah, he is obedient too," I added.

"Hey bro! Do you remember the way he barked at the other dogs? He was so furious. He is supposed to behave decently in public. He didn't listen to you at all the other day."

"Fatso! It was just a bad day. I have never seen him barking like that. It's all because of those filthy street dogs. I know Master behaves well in a crowd and doesn't easily get distracted. I think he can easily clear the obedience test."

"Hope so!" Fatso uttered. "What is the third phase?"

"Bow-bow's third phase is Protection. The dog must protect its owner when somebody attacks."

"Oh!"

"In this exercise, I want you to be the one who attacks me, and Master should bite you to protect me."

"What?! I am going home, Rahul. Bye!" Fatso was hesitant.

"Hey! I was just kidding, Fatso. Wear a padded sleeve on your left arm and hide somewhere. I'll ask Master to find you. After he finds you, try to pretend to attack me, and then Master will jump on you and bite the padded sleeve so you won't be hurt."

"Bro! I'm still afraid."

"Come on, Fatso! I'll be right beside you. Once Master attacks, you can gently tap him with a bamboo stick to test his courage."

"Oh no! I feel so sorry for him. What if he gets hurt?"

"Yeah, that's where the real test lies. If Master can dodge the blows and doesn't give up the attack, and continues to fight despite the blows, then he would surely pass the test," I explained.

"Blows to pass the test?! That's so sad for him."

Fatso didn't do exactly as I had instructed him to do, so we had to rush to the hospital.

"Dude! I asked you to show the padded sleeve to Master, not your bare arm!" I shouted. Fatso was in tears and said, "I will never ever do Bow-bow training again in my life."

• • •

CHAPTER VII

A Walk Along The Seashore

It was a Sunday evening, and I didn't choose to play. Once again, I had the desire to go to the beach. So, I walked alongside Master through the riverside until we reached the ocean. Memories started flooding back to me, but dwelling on the past and her beautiful face was not my intention. In that moment, all I wanted was to be myself, fully present, and cherish every single moment.

Master strolled along the seashore, leaving his tiny footprints in the sand. As I journeyed along life's shore, I wondered if I would be able to make a lasting impact. Could my small marks serve as guidance to those who would follow in my footsteps? Without hesitation, I left my own footprint on the briny sand. The next moment, it was the ocean's turn to dissolve and erase it. Eventually, I realized that even though I may leave a mark in my life, someday it will be wiped away and dissolved, with no memories of it remaining. So, why should I bother leaving a mark?

I witnessed gigantic waves that appeared invincible, commanding both fear and admiration from those around. Can I choose to be as invincible as those waves in order to gain respect and fame? Can I become unconquerable? All my dreams faded away when the seemingly invincible waves crashed and became one with the sea. The waves I had admired and adored were no more. Despite my appearance of invincibility, a day will come when I am merely a dream. So, why should I bother to be powerful and invincible?

The world's knowledge is as vast as the sea. How can I possibly absorb this unfathomable ocean? How does one attain knowledge of all the complex subjects in the world? As I stared at the horizon, a realization struck me: one doesn't need to drink the entire sea to know that it is salty! A single drop of briny water is enough to bring about realization. But where do I find that drop of knowledge? Everything appears to be a fleeting illusion. Who can I rely on when the world has abandoned me? Then, I found solace when I noticed a shadow passing by. Somehow, I knew that HE was the man who always stood by my side. But even so, everything is ephemeral. My own shadow deserted me when darkness fell. Whom can I trust now?

My eyes gazed toward the dark sky, searching for a light, and I found myself engulfed in darkness. Then, a smile graced my face as I discovered what I had been seeking. Yes, it was those twinkling stars that taught me the true meaning. Only those luminous objects, which radiate independently without relying on others, are the ones that leave a lasting impact and possess boundless knowledge.

After all, even the stars eventually fade away. Nevertheless, it was worth taking a stroll along the seashore.

• • •

The murder mystery haunted me day and night. The reason for my intense involvement was Master. If I could assist the police in uncovering any clues, I could attribute it solely to Master's assistance. I was aware that entering the dog show wouldn't be effective since the judges wouldn't allow a handicapped dog to compete. In search of a clue, I made my way to the police station. Master had discovered Elena's body, adding a new track to the murder mystery, and the police appreciated our efforts in aiding them.

"Hello, sir," I greeted Suresh, the sub-inspector of police. He was engrossed in going through the files. If my school books were as thick as those files, I would never even dare to touch them. I had heard that he was a very sincere and honest man in the department, and people were always welcome to meet him for assistance. In the present times, fear enveloped a common man when stepping into a police station. Amongst such corrupt officials, Suresh was definitely an outlier.

"Hello, Rahul," he greeted back with a smile. "What a surprise! What brings you here, my boy?" he asked. I was glad that someone like him remembered me when my own class teacher forgot me at times.

"Just felt like dropping by to say hello, sir. Sorry if I am interrupting."

"Not at all. Tell me, how have you been?" he asked politely.

"I am fine, sir. Thank you. How about you?" I tried to match his politeness.

"I am doing well. Fortunately, I am not one of the victims of these files," he chuckled, pointing at the file he was going through. Every day they encountered crimes, and it was always a risky business when one was honest.

"Sir, have you found any clues about Elena's murder and Pooja's missing case?" I asked curiously.

"Hmmm. Not yet, Rahul," he sighed.

"It is said that the criminal will always leave behind some clue, no matter how clever they are," I remarked, feeling like a detective.

"You're right, my friend. Just imagine going out at night, stabbing a random passerby with no connection to you, and running away after snatching their valuables. What clues can you guess would be left in that situation? There are cases where murderers leave clues, but we fail to notice them because there aren't many factors linking the victim and the culprit," he explained.

He seemed to be making a valid point, but I wasn't convinced.

"What about the scent trails he leaves behind, sir?" I suggested.

"Yeah, maybe we could have traced it, but the body was found one month after the rape," he responded.

"Rape?!" I exclaimed in surprise.

"The post-mortem analysis revealed that she was raped," he confirmed.

"Oh no! Then the semen sample could have confirmed his identity, am I right, sir?" I briefly utilized my knowledge of biology in real life, something I never thought I would need until I got married.

"The body has decayed, and obtaining a semen sample at this stage is difficult," he explained.

"Then how did they confirm that she was raped?"

"Nobody removes the victim's clothes after murdering them. The killer must have done it before raping her and then brutally killing her. The absence of clothes in the pit suggests that he may have committed such an act," he elaborated.

"Oh!" I responded, processing the information.

"Yeah, Rahul."

"Sir, do you mind if I go through the investigation file? I'll see if I can find something," I asked, trying to sound promising.

His laughter made me feel intimidated. Why does everyone think I'm just a kid who plays with a dog?

"Yeah, you can take a look at it," he said, instructing the constable to bring me the file. I could sense his lack of trust in my ability to find a clue.

The constable brought a stack of files, and just by looking at them, I felt like I was being punished. If a teacher had given me so many assignments, I would have felt overwhelmed. But this time, it was my choice to go through them. I was stunned as I looked at all the files, but I wasn't afraid.

I carefully examined every detail. Numerous people had provided their statements, including my classmates, Elena's friends, and even the Bungalow man. I wondered how the police had located him in the first place. He could be the murderer, cleverly evading detection. I read through the files the entire day without taking a break. After five hours of extensive study, Suresh called me.

"It's already late, Rahul! Please leave soon," he said, sounding a little angry.

"Okay, sir," I obediently replied.

The thought that continuously occupied my mind was why Elena's boyfriend hadn't been interrogated. Where is he now?

"Rahul! What are you thinking? Don't you want to go home?" he asked.

I simply smiled at him, bid him goodbye, and walked away. I knew I had found the culprit, but I needed more time to prove it.

• • •

As the holidays came to a close, the school once again became a bustling hive of activity. The hallways that had been silent and empty during the break now reverberated with the sounds of eager chatter and hurried footsteps.

Excitement filled the air as students reunited with their friends and settled back into the rhythm of school life.

Stepping into the familiar classroom, I found myself surrounded by the hum of animated conversations. The room was alive with the energy of students catching up on their holiday adventures and sharing stories of their escapades.

Taking my usual place at the back of the class, I joined my trusted companions, Fatso and Arvind. Despite any reservations I may have had about Fatso, he remained a loyal friend who had seen me through countless school days.

"What's up, buddy?" I inquired, noticing that Arvind seemed lost in his thoughts.

"Everything's fine, bro. How were your holidays?" he asked.

"Superb! How about yours?"

"I'm glad to have gotten over this headache," Arvind replied, looking better than he did a few months ago.

As usual, Fatso was engrossed in gobbling down bananas like there was no tomorrow. It seemed like he had made a miraculous recovery from the dog bite. The bite had been mild, sparing him from any major harm. "So, Fatso, how's the 'bow-bow' treatment treating you?" I playfully quipped, expecting a witty response. However, Fatso remained silent, his mouth too occupied with the constant chewing. I couldn't help but wonder if those thirty-two teeth of his had committed some serious sin to end up in Fatso's mouth. It seemed like he was on duty 24/7, devoted to his never-ending feast.

"Shh... shh... shhh..." Fatso struggled to speak.

"Schutzhund, Schutzhund!" I prompted, trying to get him to pronounce it correctly. "Never speak of it ever again.

Nobody must know how I got bitten. Let's keep it a secret," he demanded.

"Okay, buddy. I understand," I replied, playing along with his seriousness.

Turning to Arvind, I asked, "Do you know about Schutzhund training?" Fatso continued to watch us, his eyes fixed on the food he was munching.

"Huh? No, I've never heard of it," Arvind innocently replied.

"Don't you know about Schutzhund?" I repeated, pretending as if it were common knowledge. Fatso stared at me with a look that said he would devour me if I didn't shut my mouth.

"Bro! Please, don't you dare tell anybody," Fatso threatened.

"What's going on, Rahul?" Arvind became curious, and soon Gopesh and Nizam gathered around.

"What's happening, guys?" Nizam asked.

"Don't you all know about Schutzhund training?" I questioned everyone.

"No," they replied in unison.

I proceeded to narrate the whole story, and as usual, Fatso ended up in tears again. Everyone in the class burst into laughter.

"Bow-wow, bow-wow!" Nizam teased Fatso, imitating a dog.

Just as we were still teasing Fatso, the class teacher walked in, providing Fatso with some much-needed relief from the embarrassment. In a low voice, I reassured him, "Don't cry, Fatso. I'll buy you Snickers after school." He smiled and wiped away his tears.

That evening, after fulfilling my promise of buying Fatso Snickers, I shared, "Yesterday, I went to the police station and spoke to the sub-inspector about the case."

"Oh! By the way, Rahul, I forgot to tell you something," Fatso interjected.

"What is it? I know you would like to go for bow-bow training once again," I teased him playfully.

"Stop kidding, bro. It's something that might help you with the murder case. I overheard my father discussing it." Fatso replied

"Oh! What is it?" I became instantly intrigued.

"Guess what? Elena's boyfriend is the sub-inspector's brother-in-law."

"What?!" My jaw dropped in disbelief.

• • •

In my house, there was a doll—a doll filled with love. Not a single day has passed in the last two years without me stealing a glance at it. It was the doll into which I poured all my love. It happened two years ago...

"May I come in, ma'am?" I asked as I approached the classroom. It was the final day of school, and I held a small gift in my hand. Quietly, I took my seat at my desk and stole a quick glance at her. She was engaged in lively conversation with her friends, laughing and inquiring about the items they had brought for the surprise game promised by the teacher that day. Everyone had been asked to bring something as a parting souvenir, a token of friendship to commemorate the memorable days we had spent together.

Everybody was eagerly waiting, wondering what the surprise game would be. Time seemed to crawl by, dragging on like a sluggish snail. Finally, the teacher's voice broke through the suspense, instructing us to rearrange the desks and form a circle. The once orderly classroom transformed into a bustling symphony of shuffling benches, creating a makeshift stage for the impending excitement.

Yet, amidst the clamor and commotion, my senses tuned in to the steady rhythm of my own heartbeat, resonating like a tribal drum deep within my chest. The anticipation reached its crescendo as the circle took shape, and there she stood, directly across from me. Clutching her tiny gift adorned with a radiant, shimmering pink wrapper, she emanated an aura of anticipation and mystery.

With a mischievous glint in her eyes, the teacher exclaimed, "Prepare yourselves for a musical exchange of surprises! I will play some music, and everyone can begin passing the gifts you have brought. When I stop the music, whoever is holding whosoever gift gets to keep them. Do we all understand the rules?" Excitement rippled through the classroom.

The enchanting notes of music floated through the air, signaling the start of the exhilarating exchange. Gifts flowed like a river, passing eagerly from one person to the next, as if guided by an invisible current of excitement. Each touch and transfer held the promise of a hidden treasure, and the room buzzed with whispers of curiosity and silent hopes.

As the melody stopped, I found myself empty-handed and noticed that many others hadn't received a gift, while a few of them held two gifts in their hands. A pang of disappointment coursed through me, but the teacher swiftly intervened, her voice filled with gentle guidance. "Guys, you're passing too quickly! Please pass slowly and one at a time so that everyone can receive a gift,"

The music began again, and the passing resumed, but this time, it was slower and more deliberate. One by one, the gifts made their way around the circle. As the music wove its spell, seemingly transcending the boundaries of time, I surrendered to the magic of the game, it felt as if the passing would continue indefinitely, a harmonious dance that united us all in friendship and celebration.

The music abruptly ceased, and there I stood, holding a gift. Uncertainty lingered as I examined the pink wrapping, similar to the ones chosen by most of the girls. Eager to unveil the surprise, I dashed back to my desk, my heart pounding with anticipation. Oh, how I hoped it would be hers!

I eagerly tore open the gift. Lo and behold, nestled within the vibrant wrapping was a stunningly alluring doll, so exquisite that any boy would keep it at one arm's distance away. As I grappled with my internal debate of whether to inquire or not, her mischievous friend approached, her voice filled with intrigue. "Hey, by any chance, is that the paper clip gift? You won't believe what she said about it!"

Before I could respond, her friend's eyes widened in disbelief as she caught sight of the doll in my possession. "Oh, my goodness! That's HER gift! She was raving about the cutest doll she had bought. You lucky!" The temptation grew stronger as her friend couldn't resist suggesting an exchange, convinced that a boy would have no use for such a doll. But I, on cloud nine with my triumph, swiftly declined the offer.

The classroom buzzed with sentimental farewells, damp eyes, and exchanged goodbyes. Amidst the emotional whirlwind, the pages of slam books filled with heartfelt messages and promises to keep in touch.

As I made my way home, my heart brimmed with delight, knowing the sweet victory I had achieved. Joy mingled with a tinge of sadness, leaving me with an unforgettable memory of that final day.

The doll found its cherished spot both in the living room's showcase and within the depths of my heart. Such was my possessiveness towards it that I guarded it fiercely, forbidding even my little sister from laying a finger upon it.

"Is anyone home?" echoed the voice of a little girl from beyond the gate. She was the daughter of the local mason. "What brings you here?" I asked. Her tiny thumb found solace in her mouth, signaling her thirst. "Come in" I invited her. After settling her into a seat, I hastened to fetch a glass of water. Upon my return, I caught sight of her captivated gaze fixed upon the enchanting doll resting in the showcase.

"Here you go, drink it up" I suggested, attempting to divert her attention from the doll. She eagerly consumed the water, yet her eyes inevitably returned to the doll's splendor. "May I play with that doll, please, brother?" she pleaded with a tone capable of melting even the hardest of hearts. Hope shimmered in her innocent eyes, mirroring the same longing I had experienced when I desired the gift. Though I initially intended to refuse her, I found myself surrendering to her innocent request, handing over the prized doll.

"Take it," I declared, granting her ownership. Pure elation washed over her, as she leaped with uncontainable joy, reminding of my own jubilation upon discovering the doll's rightful owner two years prior.

Love is not the way where you keep everything in your bay. It is a way where you give everything away.

• • •

We impatiently awaited the arrival of our class teacher during the first hour. Miss Priya, our English teacher, gracefully entered the classroom. She possessed an ethereal beauty that seemed to transcend the boundaries of our school. The mere presence of this enchanting educator was a treat for our senses. With bated breath, the boys vied for a fleeting glimpse of her, their eyes fixated on the alluring folds of her elegantly draped sari. As she moved, heads turned like synchronized satellites, desperate to capture every mesmerizing moment.

"I have an announcement to make," she said in her sweet and dreamy voice. No one was interested in the announcement; all eyes were fixed on what seemed like the eighth wonder of the world.

"We have a final debate in two days. The winner will be determined in this finale." The mere mention of the upcoming spectacle electrified the atmosphere, igniting a whirlwind of hushed whispers and excited murmurs. This debate was no ordinary affair; it had been two long years since a winner had last been crowned, making it a momentous occasion. The competition itself was a unique concept, seldom embraced by other schools. The entire school would be watching the finale, as it aimed to encourage students to think beyond just the curricular activities.

"The topic is," Priya madam raised her voice to unveil, "Did Gandhi's path uplift the outcast people, or did Ambedkar's fight for the poor achieve the same?"

"Huh?" I murmured to Fatso, "Such a political concept."

The debate between Gandhi and Ambedkar had been a fiery topic in the news. TV shows were abuzz with debates over who truly fought for the impoverished.

"Our chief guest will be a freedom fighter who fought alongside Gandhiji," announced Ma'am, "and the Chairman of the Dalit Welfare Committee of the state."

"Bro, why are they making it so political?" Fatso rebelled. "They should have chosen a topic more relevant to our age."

"Fatso, they likely selected it because it's the current hot news," I tried to calm him down.

"To be honest, I barely know much about these figures, Gandhi and Ambedkar, except for the fact that they fought for our freedom."

After briefly providing details about the upcoming debate, Priya madam left the classroom. Instantly, our discussion halted, and our gaze followed her graceful departure. The lingering scent of her presence gradually faded, and we returned to our senses.

"Do you think we stand a chance of winning, Rahul?" Gopesh asked.

"I don't know," I replied.

When she was still with us, we were leading the competition, and it seemed almost certain that our team would claim the title this year. However, once she departed, we found ourselves without anyone to challenge and speak up. The opposing team effortlessly surpassed us with their exceptional ability to score points. Ramesh, the strongest contender from the opposing team, had become increasingly impulsive in the past few months. He was also the anchor for the school festival, unmatched in his skill to deliver a speech effectively.

"Rahul, even if we may not excel in the art of oration, I believe we can defeat them by selecting the right content and ensuring the active participation of every team member," urged Gopesh.

Points were awarded for various categories, including content, style, delivery, participation of team members, and the ability to sway the audience.

"I will win this debate for all of you," I promised my friends and fellow team members.

"How?" Gopesh inquired.

"I'm not entirely sure yet, but it was her desire for our team to emerge victorious in this competition, and I shall make it a reality."

• • •

121

CHAPTER VIII

The Final Debate

Since I had limited knowledge about the political conflict between Ambedkar and Gandhi, I spent the whole day within the walls of our library. Immersed in the vast sea of historical literature, unravelling the intricate stories of these two great personalities. The final period came to a close, signalling the end of my scholarly pursuits for the day.

With a desire to delve deeper into their lives, I requested the librarian to extend the closing time for just one more hour. He regretfully refused, informing me of his pre-arranged plans. Determined to make the most of the limited time available, I resorted to borrowing two precious volumes with just one day left to finish reading them.

I was on my way back home, accompanied by Fatso and two fat books in my hands. "Bro! Did you find any pointers for the debate?" Fatso inquired.

"I've been diving into their life histories, but I'm still undecided about what to present," I replied.

"Bro, why is there a conflict between them in the first place?" Fatso asked curiously.

"It's quite a lengthy tale, Fatso, and it's the same old one," I said.

"Do you want to explain now, or should I wait for tomorrow's debate?" he asked.

He seemed hungry, not for food, so I began to explain, "Gandhi hailed from a high-caste family, comprising only about 10-15% of the total population, and they held sway over all of India, much like the English did in South Africa.

On the other hand, Ambedkar was born into a Dalit family, considered untouchables and subjected to historical humiliation. These Dalits never enjoyed the privileges that the wealthy experienced."

"So, it's a battle between the rich and the poor?" Fatso questioned, seeking clarification.

"Not precisely, Fatso, but yes, in a way. It's much more intricate than that," I responded.

"Like what?" Fatso probed further.

"These Dalits endured inhumane suppression for years until Ambedkar emerged as the first educated Dalit in India. He fought for his people's representation and urged the British to grant them autonomy, the ability to govern themselves. So, after widespread protests and political upheaval, the British agreed to the Dalits' demands. In elections, only a Dalit could elect a Dalit representative, ensuring their representation in society. However, Gandhi opposed this approach."

"Why?" Fatso asked, curiously.

"Gandhi believed that the British were employing a 'divide and rule' policy. He argued that if Dalits voted only for Dalit representatives, Hindus voted for Hindu representatives, and Muslims voted for Muslim representatives, it would fracture society and hinder unity, as each community would pursue its own interests."

"Hmm," Fatso sighed, contemplating the complexities of the situation.

"In order to bring unity and bypass the election process, Gandhi resorted to a hunger strike, which he continued till his requests were met. Ultimately, Ambedkar agreed with Gandhi, but under one condition," I continued.

"What condition?" Fatso seemed deeply engaged in the conversation.

"Ambedkar insisted on reservations for Dalits proportionate to their population, approximately 15-18%," I explained.

"So, it sounds like a compromise. Both sides had their concerns addressed. Why does the issue persist then? Why are they still dragging it?" Fatso queried.

"Some sections of the underdeveloped Dalit community believe that the English-devised system of separate electorates should have been implemented, as it would have provided them with better positions. They hold Gandhi responsible for obstructing their goals," I responded.

"I see," Fatso nodded in understanding.

"On the other hand, higher-caste individuals feel deprived of the benefits of reservations. Sometimes, their merit is disregarded in order to fulfil the reservation criteria. They blame Ambedkar for such setbacks," I elaborated.

"So, these differences are the root cause of this ongoing melodrama?" Fatso summarized.

"Yes. However, there is something that these two legends share in common," I hinted.

"What is it?" Fatso asked eagerly.

"That, my friend, is something I am yet to discover," leaving him intrigued and eager for more.

• • •

The next day, I immersed myself in further exploration of these remarkable individuals. However, the elusive common thread that connected them still eluded me. Upon returning home, I ventured out for a walk with my faithful companion, Master. I wished I had my angel by my side to answer all my seemingly foolish inquiries. Master always compensated for her absence. Every time I looked at

Master, I saw glimpses of her. In my eyes, Master was the vessel through which she spoke to me, or so I believed.

Master had transformed from being just a dog; now, he embodied my reflection. As we strolled, memories flooded my mind of the day I first laid eyes on him. Little did I know then that Master would become my closest confidant, my unwavering companion. I reminisced about the days when I used to hold him tightly by my side, watching over him. Now, Master was free to roam, but in truth, he was still my master.

As we approached the beach, I caught sight of sculptures depicting the valiant freedom fighters. Gandhi, Nehru, Ambedkar, Vallabhai Patel, and many others stood proudly. Master ventured forward and positioned himself between the statues of Gandhi and Ambedkar. I couldn't fathom the message Master was trying to convey, but I found myself captivated by the idols, gazing upon them intently.

There stood an old man upon a granite pedestal, emanating youthful energy in his movement while exuding tranquility in his thoughts. With a fragile stick in his hand, he possessed an indomitable spirit. Clad in nothing but the attire of dignity, he was Gandhi—the man who discarded his clothes to wage a battle against bloodshed.

Beside him stood another towering personality on a similar pedestal, his gaze focused and his stance resolute. The Constitution rested firmly in his hand, symbolizing the foundation of India's future. Behind his spectacles lay a vision that extended far beyond the present, while his tailored attire inspired millions of impoverished souls. He was Ambedkar—the man of unblemished character and unquestionable integrity.

Beneath these moral figures, I stood contemplatively, pondering their significance. One had forsaken the desire for material garments, while the other donned an exquisite, formal English suit.

Why do famous personalities choose divergent paths that complicate the understanding for their followers? Why does one embrace simplicity while the other embraces aristocracy? As I fixated my gaze upon them, my thoughts delved deeper into contemplation... What should I make of this? And then, my voice resounded, "Aren't they essentially the same?"

Gandhi, born into royalty, willingly cast aside his aristocratic attire to become one with the impoverished, conveying the message that a wealthy individual could embody the humility of a poor man. On the other hand, Ambedkar, hailing from an outcast family, shattered social barriers and fought to stand among the elites, demonstrating that a person from humble origins could achieve wealth and success without compromising their simplicity.

"I have found my answer!" I exclaimed.

Despite the contrasting paths taken by these remarkable personalities, their minds converge on shared intentions.

• • •

Finally, the debate came to an end. Everyone surrounding me offered their congratulations. In that moment, I no longer felt like the same kid I was just a day before. Something within me had changed. We were declared the winners of the competition. It was perhaps the first time I had spoken with such conviction. I had never dreamt that I could accomplish this, and now I couldn't believe that I actually did. The sensation of victory was incredible. Riding high on cloud nine, I noticed my Principal approaching me.

"That was an excellent debate, Rahul. I've witnessed teams fiercely defending their respective positions, but you were exceptional. You managed to bridge the gap between two contrasting ideologies," my Principal praised.

"Thank you, Sir," I replied, brimming with elation.

"I am truly impressed, my son."

"Thank you, Sir. Your words mean a lot to me," I expressed gratefully.

Fatso walked towards me, handing over his Diary Milk chocolate. Never before had I seen Fatso willingly share his portion of chocolate with others in my entire life. In that moment, I felt like a blessed child.

Our team emerged as the winners, and Ramesh from the opposing team received the award for Best Speaker. Undoubtedly, he deserved the accolade. However, today was my day, and no one could take away the fulfillment of my own dreams. Applause resounded from all directions, but no one knew who had inspired me to speak in such a manner. While those around me congratulated my achievement, in my heart, I expressed gratitude to my girl and my Master. The people surrounding me might forget the words I uttered, but I will never forget the lessons taught to me by my girl and my Master.

• • •

"What is the one thing you would like to do every day?" I asked her.

"Haha, I want to eat," she chuckled.

"I mean, what is something you would love to do?" I clarified.

"Yeah, I love eating. Don't you?" She teased.

"For the first time, I am being serious, and it seems like you're just kidding," I remarked.

We were walking home after school. "Why? Don't you enjoy this role reversal? Why don't you tell me what you would like to do every day?" she responded, as she often did.

"I would like to spend the whole day with you," I whispered softly.

Once again, she burst into laughter. "Don't you feel the same way? Please stop laughing at me," I pleaded.

"Just go back a year and tell me what you liked then," she asked.

"I had a crush on Priya. I always dreamt about her," I confessed, blushing slightly.

"Haha, look at you. Your desires change every moment. How can I trust that they won't change now?" she remarked.

"Oh, no, not every moment. Well, maybe they change every year," I said thoughtfully.

Once again, she laughed. "Tell me something you want to do your whole life, something you would cherish doing."

"I don't know. I haven't discovered it yet. I love playing cricket, but I'm unsure how far I'll be able to pursue it," I admitted.

"What would you do if your dream of becoming a cricketer doesn't come true?" she asked.

"That's why I want to be with you. You know what I need to do," I replied.

She chuckled as we walked down the road. Trees, vehicles, and dust stood in silence. Only her voice echoed in my ears.

A small duck floated on the pond, occasionally dipping its neck into the water. "Look at the duck. Isn't it beautiful?" I asked, attempting to change the subject.

"What makes you say it's beautiful?" I sensed a hint of sarcasm in her tone.

"Look at its feathers, its color, the way it moves. Everything is so awesome," I found myself rambling without much

thought.

"Is that all you see?" she questioned.

"Yeah. Don't you think it's beautiful? What else do you see in it?" I inquired.

"When it couldn't fly high with its wings, it chose to swim deep into the water with them," she remarked.

"Wow! That's wonderful. Now please tell me, what would you love to do?" I pleaded.

"Just sleep peacefully," she replied.

"That's it?" I asked, puzzled, expecting a more profound answer. Just sleep?

"Yeah, your sleep symbolizes what you do. Remember that," she explained.

"But I sleep like a pig every day. What does it symbolize?"

"You'll find out someday, Rahul," she said in her usual tone. Whenever I didn't understand what she said, instead of explaining, she always left it for me and time to answer.

"One last question," I said.

"Go ahead," she smiled.

"What would you like to do on the last day of your life?" I asked.

"What?! Have you lost your mind?" she exclaimed. Just as she was about to get to that, her attention was immediately drawn to a puppy attempting to cross the road, trying to escape from the passing vehicles. Without hesitation, she rushed over to pick it up and move it to the safer side of the road.

BOOOMM!!

I jolted awake from my tormenting dream, my body drenched in cold sweat, and my breath coming in panicked gasps. There was a profound cry without a voice, and my body carried an unending void—an immense weight that shook my legs but couldn't be relieved. It was a reality that stood like a recurring dream with each passing moment.

Great personalities have the power to make their presence felt, but it is only humble human beings who can make their absence felt. She was fully present within me, yet her absence loomed in front of me.

It was the final question, the very last words I could ever utter to her. It was the moment when tragedy struck, an unforgiving minivan callously obliterating her kind heart in an instant. A raw wound that refuses to heal. If there was one moment I could erase from my memory forever, it would be this. Unfortunately, such an option eludes me, and I cannot undo what has transpired. Little did I know that it would be the last day of her life with me, or should I say, the last day of my life with her.

• • •

As the exams loomed closer, casting a shadow of stress over our 12th-grade class, a clear divide emerged. The girls diligently buried themselves in their books, while the boys seemed to have a gravitational pull towards leisure and mischief.

"I'm gonna miss you all so much, guys," Fatso expressed, his voice tinged with melodrama.

"Whoa there, Mr. Sentimental! Feeling all mushy already?" Nizam teased him, unable to resist a playful jab.

"Hey cut it out, Nizam!" Gopesh chimed in, coming to Fatso's defense.

"Why so sad, Fatso? We can still hang out after graduation. Nothing's going to change," I reassured him, attempting to lighten the mood.

Something troubled him deeply, a hidden concern he kept concealed from us.

"Guys, listen up. Brace yourselves. I'm going abroad for future studies. Off to the UK. My dad just dropped this bombshell on me yesterday," Fatso confessed, his tone heavy with sadness.

"Whoa, Fatso! That's some big news!" Nizam exclaimed, trying to inject a dose of enthusiasm into the situation.

"But I don't wanna leave this place, man. I love it here," Fatso replied, his voice tinged with a sigh.

"Oh, come on, Fatso! Don't be a baby. It's gonna be epic! Just imagine all the beautiful girls you'll encounter. Mini skirts, pencil-cut pants, it'll be a fashion fiesta!" Nizam interjected, always finding a way to lighten the mood by bringing up the topic of attractive ladies.

"And, um, will they have bananas there?" Fatso quipped, a mischievous glint in his eyes.

That was the cue for everyone to burst into laughter.

While we engaged in conversation, our principal made his grand entrance into the classroom. True to form, he delivered his lengthy speech about the importance of seriousness and focus for the upcoming final examinations. In such moments, daydreaming became our secret refuge. Although all eyes were on the principal, our minds wandered off into our own little filmy worlds. Once the principal departed, we snapped back to reality.

"Hey guys, anyone up for some video games? Nobody will be home at my place tomorrow," Fatso proposed.

However, it seemed that nobody was interested. One by one, they declined Fatso's invitation, offering various excuses.

"What about you, Rahul? Will you come?" Fatso turned to me, hopeful for at least one companion.

"Sorry, Fatso. I have some tasks to complete," I replied, regretfully declining.

"Unfortunately, Arvind is absent today," Fatso said, his disappointment evident.

"Why Arvind?" I inquired, growing curious about the situation.

"Arvind is the only one who joins me in playing video games. He's the sole enthusiast in our class," Fatso explained.

"I thought David was also quite into gaming," I stated, feeling perplexed.

"Yeah, he used to be. Unfortunately, he's no longer with us," Fatso responded sadly.

"What?!" I exclaimed, stunned by the revelation.

• • •

Throughout the entire night, sleep eluded me as I replayed the series of events that had unfolded. The intense training of Master, the tragic loss of David, Pooja's disappearance, and the gossip-filled classroom discussions—all these moments seemed to converge towards a single, undeniable conclusion. Yet, despite my relentless contemplation, I couldn't quite put all the pieces together. However, one thing I knew for certain: I knew who was responsible.

The next morning, I set out with my Master and Fatso by my side.

"Where are we headed, Rahul?" Fatso inquired, curiosity lacing his voice.

"You'll find out soon enough, Fatso," I replied, withholding the suspense.

"I have no clue what you're talking about. What will I find out?" Fatso persisted, clearly puzzled.

"The identity of David and Elena's murderer," I stated matter-of-factly.

"What? You must be joking," Fatso exclaimed, unable to believe his ears.

"No, I assure you, I'm not."

"Then who is it?" Fatso pressed for an answer.

"It's someone from our own class," I revealed, heightening the intrigue.

"You've truly lost it this time. How can one of our classmates be the murderer? I find this absurd, Rahul. Stop with the nonsense," Fatso responded, his disbelief palpable.

"Just hear me out. Remember when you mentioned that only Arvind, David, and you were the ones who frequently played video games together?" I questioned.

"Yeah, what about it? What does that have to do with anything?" Fatso asked impatiently.

"Recall that on the day of David's murder, he had called you to play games at his house. It's possible that he had also invited Arvind. And who knows, maybe Arvind went over the night before, while you could not, leading to a disastrous turn of events," I explained.

"Hmm...I can't believe this," Fatso mused, seemingly contemplating the possibility.

"Perhaps David didn't inform you about Arvind's early arrival, or maybe he didn't consider it important enough to mention," I speculated.

"That's the only clue you have, Rahul? Your reasoning seems stupid" Fatso inquired

"No, Fatso, there's more," I revealed.

"Remember when the police interrogated everyone in our class? If Arvind was truly the culprit, they would have uncovered it by now, right?" Fatso posed a logical question.

"You're correct. However, Arvind was on medical leave for a month due to his health condition," I reminded him.

"Oh, right! But didn't the police question him after he returned?" Fatso asked, seeking clarification.

"No, they didn't. When I visited the police station that day, I noticed a crucial detail," I shared.

"What was it?" Fatso pressed for more information.

"I carefully examined all the files and the remarks provided by everyone involved in the case. Surprisingly, Arvind's name was absent from the list of interrogated individuals. That's when I started to suspect him, although I couldn't be certain," I explained.

"I initially thought Elena's boyfriend might be the culprit, especially since he was related to a sub-inspector. I thought he might be receiving some protection," Fatso admitted, sharing his own line of thinking.

Naturally, it was a conclusion that most people would arrive at. Hence, the sub-inspector likely avoided excessive publicity surrounding the case. Perhaps he wanted to maintain a clean image and distance himself from it," I elaborated.

"Hmm, that could be a possibility," Fatso responded, contemplating the idea.

"Do you still have doubts about what I'm saying?" I asked, noticing the puzzled expression on his face.

"I don't know, Rahul. It's all quite confusing," Fatso admitted, his uncertainty apparent.

"Remember the other day when we were watching that movie at Gopesh's house? There was a murder scene, and you couldn't continue watching," I reminded him.

"Yes, and Arvind also seemed a bit nervous and followed me to provide company," Fatso recalled.

"Exactly. But Fatso, the difference is that you didn't watch the movie either. However, all the clues point to Arvind as the main suspect. And there's one more piece of evidence that confirms his involvement," I divulged.

"What is it?" Fatso inquired, intrigued by the newfound revelation.

A few months ago, I took Master to the spot where Elena was buried. I didn't have much hope of finding any leads since it had been a while since the murder. But that day, my Master managed to track Arvind's scent. He was barking furiously, and at the time, I mistakenly thought he was reacting to other dogs," I explained.

"Oh yes, I remember that," Fatso recollected, joining the dots.

I felt relieved that I had finally convinced him.

"But how could Master recognize Arvind's scent after such a long time?" Fatso inquired.

"Didn't I mention that scents can linger on the ground for up to a month if left undisturbed? Coupled with the cold winter climate at the time, it helped preserve the scent," I clarified.

"Master is truly incredible," Fatso commented, a smile forming on his face.

• • •

CHAPTER IX

What Lies Beyond ?

We went to Arvind's house along with Master to verify whether our theory was indeed the truth, and I was determined to find out what compelled him to commit such a heinous crime. Standing in front of Arvind's house, a place we had visited countless times before, the atmosphere was no longer filled with the warmth of friendship but instead tinged with apprehension. Each small step we took intensified the tension, as we were about to confront someone who was no longer just a friend. Arvind resided with his grandmother, while his parents lived in the city. His affection for his grandma was so strong that he never felt the absence of his parents. Standing outside the gate, we called out his name, our voices tinged with anger.

"He left a few hours ago," his grandma replied. We were left clueless about his whereabouts.

"Do you have any idea where he might have gone?" I inquired.

"He never tells me where he goes, kid. I always ask him, but he's so stubborn. He never tells me. God knows where he goes," she responded sadly.

We had no leads to follow. Impatience started to brew among us as we waited for his return.

"What should we do now?" Fatso asked, frustration evident in his voice.

"Hmm..." I pondered, searching for a solution.

"I don't see a more ingenious plan than this," I said, gesturing towards Arvind's abandoned school shoes perched by the door. With unwavering determination, I beckoned Master, my faithful companion, to inhale the scent lingering on the socks. Our pursuit resumed, and we embarked on a relentless quest to locate Arvind, vowing not to relent until we apprehended him.

Master, utilizing his remarkable olfactory abilities, led us through winding paths tracing Arvind's elusive scent with unerring precision. The journey took us beyond the confines of the village, where civilization melted away into an ancient expanse of untamed wilderness. Towering trees stood as silent sentinels, casting eerie shadows that seemed to dance with our mounting apprehension.

As we delved deeper into the depths of the forest, a palpable sense of trepidation coursed through our veins. The haunting whispers of rustling leaves and the ethereal glow of dappled sunlight only intensified our unease. Yet, we pressed on, driven by an unwavering resolve to find our lost friend.

"Fatso, can you go and bring the police? And give me your mobile phone," I said urgently.

"Sure, Rahul. I will call you once I bring them here," he replied, preparing to leave.

"Just a minute," I interjected, pausing him in his tracks. I flipped the mobile phone and examined the backside.

"Why is that for?" Fatso questioned.

"That is the IMEI code, Fatso. Hurry up! Note it down," I commanded.

"I don't have a pen to jot it down," he stuttered, frustration evident in his voice.

"Can't you memorize this 16-digit number?" I asked, skepticism creeping into my tone, aware of Fatso's questionable memory skills.

"No way. Why do we need such a lengthy number anyway? I can just call you, right?" he replied, seeking clarification.

"We are uncertain about what lies beyond. This number will assist the police in locating me if any issues arise," I explained as I scribbled the IMEI number on the sand. Afterwards, I texted the number and sent it to Nizam and Gopesh.

"That's clever, Rahul," Fatso appreciated, patting my back, and quickly ran off to bring the police.

As Master led me deeper into the woods, I grew increasingly tense. My mind was filled with a multitude of thoughts racing relentlessly. What could Arvind be doing in such a secluded location? Why did he choose to come here? Finally, after half an hour of searching, we managed to track him down.

Arvind was accompanied by three unfamiliar men, whose identities remained unknown to me. It appeared that they were under the influence of drugs, with syringes and powder scattered in their vicinity. Unaware of our presence, they continued their activities. I pondered the challenging situation—how could a boy and a dog possibly confront four? It was clear that waiting for Fatso to bring the police was the most prudent course of action. Glancing at the mobile phone, I discovered with dismay that there was no signal available for Fatso to contact me.

As I frantically sought a secure hiding spot from which to observe their actions, my heart sank as one of the men spotted me and menacingly approached. Master's gaze remained fixed on the approaching threat, his instincts honed and ready to defend us both. Sensing the imminent danger, Master lunged at the man, sinking his teeth into his arm with a ferocity reminiscent of our intense Schutzhund training sessions. This time, however, the bite was not merely a demonstration but a forceful defense. The man's agonized screams pierced the air, a desperate plea for help. I stood frozen, a spectator to the unfolding chaos. Suddenly, another one of the men swung a sturdy stick at Master, striking him forcefully. Despite the brutal assault, Master refused to release his grip. Fueled by an overwhelming desire to protect my Master, I intervened, engaging in a desperate struggle with the burly assailant. Their intoxication seemed to impair their physical strength, as they wavered unsteadily on the uneven ground, struggling to maintain their balance.

As the chaos unfolded, Arvind stumbled onto the scene, his state of intoxication evident. Oblivious to the gravity of the situation, he became the unwitting target of Master's protective instincts. With a forceful lunge, Master sank his teeth into Arvind's flesh, leaving no doubt about the severity of the situation. The sight of Master bleeding profusely from the relentless beatings inflicted upon him did nothing to diminish his commitment. In that moment, I realized the true essence of resilience and strength. Many may accomplish remarkable feats through sheer effort, but only a select few possess the fortitude to persevere even in the face of their own suffering. Master's abdomen region was bleeding profusely, inflicted by the merciless whips of the stranger. Blood trickled from its mouth, a testament to the ferocity with which it had torn apart a piece of flesh from its assailant.

Deep within me, I had witnessed Master radiating pure benevolence, but now it seemed that a profound intensity of violence had overtaken him. Perhaps, this is the true essence of a living being - the ability to mirror their nature based on the demands of the circumstances at hand.

A few minutes later, I witnessed the stranger approaching Master with a gleaming knife, a surge of panic coursed through my veins. I was frozen, caught in the grip of fear and indecision. My mind raced, desperately searching for a solution, but my body remained immobilized, as if paralyzed by the weight of the impending tragedy. The scene unfolded before me in agonizing slow motion, each passing second amplifying the intensity of the moment.

Master, weakened and injured, seemed oblivious to the imminent threat, still panting from the exertion of its previous battle. His once fierce eyes now held a glimmer of vulnerability, unaware of the danger that lurked just inches away. The stranger's hand trembled with anticipation, his malevolent intentions etched upon his face.

Time seemed to stand still as I grappled with the overwhelming urge to protect Master, to shield it from harm's way. A surge of courage welled up within me, breaking through the chains of my immobilization. In a swift and decisive motion, I lunged forward, desperately grasping the stranger's arm, diverting the trajectory of the deadly weapon. The air crackled with tension as the knife missed its intended target, its metallic edge grazing against Master's side, leaving a deep gash in its wake.

As the tensions rose, the sound of approaching sirens heralded the arrival of the police, accompanied by Fatso, our long-awaited rescuer.

• • •

The next day, I met Sub Inspector Suresh at the police station. Master was in the hospital, undergoing treatment for his injuries.

"Hi, Sir," I greeted him as I entered the room.

"Hello, Rahul. Come in. Please have a seat," Suresh invited me. After the events of yesterday, the police had successfully arrested all the men involved.

"Did he confess to murdering David and Elena?" I asked, eager to know if the truth had finally come to light.

"Hmm, yes," Suresh replied, confirming my suspicions. The culprit had indeed confessed to the murders.

A mixture of emotions washed over me—relief, sadness, and a lingering sense of justice. It was a bittersweet moment, knowing that the truth had been revealed, but also acknowledging the tragic loss of innocent lives.

"It is not just about David and Elena's murder, Rahul. There is a lot more to this case," Suresh said grimly. "This gang has been involved in even more serious crimes. All the girls who were reported missing in the neighboring villages are linked to this case."

My eyes widened in shock. "Where were they? Are they safe?"

Suresh sighed heavily. "Unfortunately, these criminals are psycho rapists. They would select a girl, gain her trust, and when the time was right, they would fulfil their sick desires and brutally kill their victims. There have been more than ten cases like this, and it appears that Arvind somehow got involved with these men and joined them in their heinous acts. One of the gang members is a wanted drug peddler"

I couldn't believe what I was hearing. Arvind, who had once been a kind and friendly person, had become part of this monstrous gang. The weight of betrayal and disbelief settled heavily upon me. It was difficult to comprehend how someone I had considered a friend could be responsible for such horrific crimes.

"On the night when David's murder took place, Arvind and one of his gang members went to David's house. It turned out that David had invited Arvind to play video games. Both Arvind and his partner in crime were under the influence of drugs," Suresh stated, not willing to delve into the details of their heinous acts.

"I can imagine what happened next," I added, my reluctance evident in my voice. The thought of the sinister events that unfolded that night was unsettling, and I preferred not to dwell on the gruesome specifics.

"So, did you find any clue about Pooja Sir?" I asked, my voice filled with concern and anticipation.

Suresh sighed heavily before responding, his expression conveying the weight of the revelation. "Yes, unfortunately, Pooja is one of their victims as well. They have buried her in the same place where you found them yesterday."

My heart sank at the news, overwhelmed with sorrow and empathy for Fatso. The thought of him learning about Pooja's fate and the pain it would cause him was unbearable.

"How is Master's condition, Rahul?" he asked, trying to divert the topic.

"Master is doing fine. Just a few injuries. The doctor says the wounds are deep, but he will recover soon."

"I'm glad to hear that. I was really impressed with the way he helped us in this investigation. In fact, without Master, we wouldn't have caught them," he said, delighted.

"Thank you, sir."

"Can I give you a suggestion?"

"Sure."

"The service of a dog like Master is essential for the police department. Master is all over today's newspaper. He is no longer just a dog."

"Yeah."

"I will give you the details of my friend who works in the defence department in the city. Go to him and talk to him. He might help you in making Master a police dog."

My happiness knew no bounds. I had never told Suresh about my dream to make Master a police dog. When the time is right, whatever we desire comes to us. I noted down the details.

• • •

After couple of weeks had passed, and Master had made significant progress in his recovery, I embarked on a journey to meet Anderson, the esteemed Associate Director of the Recruitment & Training Department. Suresh had graciously recommended that I seek Anderson's assistance in the noble endeavor of inducting Master into the prestigious department. Accompanied by Fatso and our Master, we embarked on our expedition in Fatso's car, ready to pave the way for Master's future as a distinguished member of the force.

We had arrived at the prestigious institute renowned for its exceptional dog training programs. It was known for providing some of the finest dogs in the country. As I entered the premises with Master by my side, a sense of pride and gratitude filled my heart. I had heard stories about how this institute collected semen samples from the best dogs around the world, meticulously bred and trained them to perfection. The dogs that graduated from this institution held immense value and were held in high regard.

"Excuse me, are you Mr. Anderson?" I inquired politely, approaching a gentleman seated at a desk. Noticing the nameplate displayed on his desk, I was hopeful that I had found the right person.

"Yes, I am. What can I assist you with?" he responded, his tone displaying a hint of curiosity.

"Sir, my name is Rahul. I believe Inspector Suresh might have already informed you about me," I introduced myself, hoping that my purpose for being there would be recognized.

"Oh, yes. He did mention your name and your dog, 'Master,' if I recall correctly," he acknowledged, his memory triggered by Inspector Suresh's recent communication.

With a smile, I confirmed, "Yes, sir. Master is patiently waiting outside the office."

"Please wait a moment," Anderson replied, excusing himself from the desk. He disappeared into his chamber briefly before returning and gesturing for us to accompany him outside to see the dog.

"I have heard a lot about your dog and have read a few articles in the newspaper lately. It's quite impressive for a dog that is not trained by professionals," he said, amazed.

"Thank you, sir," I replied, filled with pride. We both exited the office and went to see Master, who was with Fatso beside the car.

"It is such a beautiful gift for a dog with only one leg," Anderson said, tapping on Master's head.

As he ran his hands over Master's head, his gaze shifted to the rubber collar, which had a steel engraving around Master's neck, and he asked, "Where did you find this dog?" There was a hint of disbelief in his voice when he took another deeper look at the imprinting on the collar. Unsure of how to respond, I paused for a moment, contemplating my answer.

"I found him on the streets in my town," I replied, fabricating a story to conceal the true origins of Master.

"Can you come back tomorrow? I would like to have Master with me. I need to discuss this with my senior, Richard," he requested hiding something he knew.

"Sure, Sir. I hope you don't mind if I play with Master for a while before leaving," I requested Anderson.

"By all means, I have no objection. You can spend some time in the field outside," replied Anderson, showing us the path to the open field where the dogs were kept freely. Each dog had its own spacious cage, allowing them to move around and play. Kennels were provided in each cage for resting, and cleanliness was meticulously maintained. It was undoubtedly one of the best environments a dog could have anywhere in the country.

"Fatso, do you like to say anything to Master. Probably, we will never be able to play like the way we played with him all these days" I asked Fatso with a tinge of sadness in my voice.

Fatso, who had been joyful all this time, suddenly comprehended the reality that Master would no longer be there to play, a wave of sadness washed over him. He stood there motionless, unable to fully grasp what lay ahead.

With his eyes moist and filled with a mix of love and longing, Fatso opened the stash of snacks he had bought. Without hesitation, he opened each packet and, one by one, fed them to Master.

"I have nothing to say Rahul, I am happy for him" he said, kissing Master on his forehead.

Overwhelmed by the emotional roller coaster, I couldn't hold back my emotions any longer. I gently ran my fingers through Master's neck and caressed his entire body. I hugged him tightly, cherishing every moment we had left together. Tears streamed down my face as I showered him with kisses, dotting his face with affection. In response,

Master licked all over my face.

"Don't worry, Master. There are other dogs here for your company, and Anderson will take care of you," I spoke to the Master. But in turn, all I received was a lick on my face.

"Don't be disheartened that you don't have a leg and can't jump like other dogs. Remember what my angel had told me: When a duck couldn't fly high with its wings, it chose to swim deep into the water with them. Even though you may not have a leg, you have a heart that has the sensitivity to touch all lives," I spoke the last words to my Master before leaving.

• • •

The next morning Anderson was in Richard's chamber, who was the director of the department.

"Sir, I have some crucial information to share with you," Anderson insisted, hoping to catch his attention.

"I have other pressing matters to attend to. Can't it wait?" Richard replied, sounding slightly annoyed.

"Sir, I believe this is of utmost urgency. It won't take much of your time," Anderson urged, emphasizing the importance of my revelation.

"Very well, Anderson. Spit it out," Richard sighed, giving him a brief moment to explain.

"Sir, approximately two and a half years ago, we received a semen sample of Brit, the renowned police dog from Scotland," .

"Yes, I recall that. Get to the point," Richard interrupted, eager to grasp the significance of his statement.

"We had the intention of breeding one of the finest dogs for investigative work," Anderson continued. "And Brit, being an exceptional police dog, was an ideal choice. He has a remarkable record, having assisted Scotland Yard in solving over 1000 cases."

Richard nodded, recalling the impressive reputation of Brit. "Yes, I remember. He was truly exceptional. In fact, one of the best in the world"

"Well, sir, using Brit's semen sample, we successfully bred a dog," Anderson revealed. "However, when the dog was young, a tragic accident occurred. A heavy iron rod fell on its leg, causing it to lose one of its limbs."

Richard's face showed no recollection of this event. "I don't recall that incident," he stated matter-of-factly.

"You had instructed us to abandon the dog on the streets," Anderson informed him.

Richard's tone turned cold as he replied, "What good is a dog with only three legs?"

"Sir, have you happened to see the newspaper clippings from last week?" Anderson asked, pointing to the article featuring Master.

"Yes, it's been all over the news," Richard responded.

"Master is the very same dog we left on the streets," Anderson revealed, a note of astonishment in his voice.

"Oh, is that so?" Richard's interest was piqued.

"Yes, sir. I was able to find out with the steel engravings on the rubber collar, which has a unique number for each dog. The owner who has been caring for Master came to us yesterday, expressing their willingness to hand over the dog," Anderson explained.

Richard's face lit up. "Well, in that case, we can gladly accept him into our institute."

"But, sir, there's more to it than just acquiring a dog," Anderson continued." I conducted a DNA sample analysis on Master, and the results revealed an exceptionally high level of intelligence. I also conducted various tests to assess his capabilities and intelligence, and the results were truly astounding. I have never encountered a dog with such remarkable intelligence. Having him as part of our institute could bring great recognition and acclaim."

Richard nodded, acknowledging the significance of the discovery. "That is indeed excellent news, Anderson. You have my full support to proceed with it. I see no objections to having Master join our institute."

• • •

CHAPTER X

Who Is The Bungalow Man ?

As I contemplated my Master's future and the realization of my girl's dream through him, a bittersweet feeling overwhelmed me. While I knew that our days of strolling together on the streets and playing as we used to were coming to an end, there was a deep sense of fulfilment in allowing him to pursue his greater purpose.

However, amidst the excitement and emotions, one question continued to haunt me: Who was the man in the bungalow? If he wasn't the one responsible for Elena's & Pooja's murder, then who was he? And why did everyone exhibit fear in his presence? The mystery surrounding this enigmatic figure lingered in my mind, urging me to seek answers and unravel the truth behind his identity and the fear associated with him.

It was 6:30 in the evening, and the darkness was slowly enveloping the fading daylight. Stepping outside, I found myself fixated on the bungalow that seemed to beckon me, enticing me to unravel the countless unanswered questions that lingered in my mind.

Usually, I tend to skip many questions during exams, unconcerned about the potential loss of marks. However, when it came to this particular question, I couldn't bear to ignore it. Who was this enigmatic Bungalow man? With a resolute determination, I left the comfort of my home and set off towards the mysterious bungalow, driven by an unwavering desire to uncover the truth, no matter what obstacles awaited me.

As I stepped outside my house, I noticed a group of children hurling stones at a peculiar-looking stranger. His unkempt hair and tattered clothes gave him an appearance of a deranged individual. It was reminiscent of the way the kids had targeted the bungalow man before, but now, their attention had shifted to this new stranger.

"Stop throwing stones at him!" I shouted at the children, unable to tolerate their cruel actions.

One of the children, their eyes filled with a mixture of disgust and fear, responded, "He's a scary man. Who knows what he's capable of? We have to chase him away before he takes us to some dark world."

Their words conveyed a deep-rooted apprehension and prejudice against the stranger, fueled by the unknown and the rumors circulating among them.

"No, he won't. He simply lacks proper clothing, but that doesn't make him dangerous. Please, stop hurting him," I pleaded with the children, trying to reason with their fears.

"But my mother told me to stay away from strange and unusual people," the kid responded, torn between what they had been taught and their natural curiosity.

Children possess incredible imaginations, capable of conjuring up extraordinary tales and theories about the world around them. However, they can also be susceptible to superstitions and their own interpretations of people and situations. It's a common trait, and I couldn't help but reflect on my own childhood, when I too was afraid of approaching abandoned houses and believed in unbelievable stories.

Time has a way of changing our minds and beliefs, revealing the irrationality of our earlier fears. It's both amusing and enlightening to observe how our perspectives evolve with experience and maturity.

After persuading the children to return to their homes, I approached the bungalow and stood near its imposing gate. The weight of it seemed to bear down on me, as if mirroring the weight of my own apprehensions. Overgrown vines and creepers twisted their way around the iron bars, adding to the eerie atmosphere. For so long, the sight of the gate had filled me with fear and kept me at bay. I had constructed my own imaginative world, conjuring up all sorts of possibilities of what might lie beyond its threshold.

But today, I was determined to shed my fears and confront the unknown. With a deep breath, I pushed open the gate. At that moment, I couldn't help but relate to those children who were governed by their own imaginations and fears. Age alone does not dictate maturity; it is the state of our minds, our willingness to confront our fears and challenge our preconceived notions.

As I rapped my knuckles against the main door, my heart pounded in my chest, the rush of adrenaline urging me to face my fear head-on. To my surprise, the door swung open easily, revealing a darkness that enveloped the house. Only a faint glow emitted from a solitary lamp in a room across the hall. With the dim illumination, I could make out the neatness and orderliness of the house. Paintings adorned the walls, and everything appeared to be in its rightful place. It was far from the unusual scene I had anticipated.

Curiosity propelled me towards the room from which the light emanated, each step taken cautiously. Through the partially ajar door, I caught sight of a figure seated on a mat, facing the wall. The sight before me was almost inconceivable, and I couldn't trust my own eyes. The mind, it seemed, possessed a stronger ability to imprint images than mere visual perception. The room exuded an air of tranquility and serenity, and there he was, the old man, engrossed in meditation. How could this person, whom I had assumed to be nefarious, radiate a sense of profound peace that transcended mere words?

I yearned to call out to him, to unleash the barrage of questions that had haunted me for days—about his true nature, the source of fear among the residents of the colony, and the connection to Master. Patiently, I waited for him to conclude his meditation, my gaze fixated upon his weathered face, marked by numerous scars I had observed months earlier. While trying to maneuver for a better vantage point, I accidentally stumbled over a flower vase, causing a sudden noise that roused the man from his introspection.

• • •

At the orphanage, Shwetha was having a heartfelt conversation with Mother Prathibha Bai, whose health was deteriorating day by day.

With a heavy heart, Shwetha shared the news, "Ma, the bank officials came today..."

Mother Prathibha Bai's face showed a mix of concern and understanding. "Hmmm, I can only imagine what they must have said."

Tears welled up in Shwetha's eyes as she continued, "They demanded the pending loan amount to be paid within 3 days, or else... we would have to vacate the place."

A wave of sadness washed over Mother Prathibha Bai as she understood the uncertain future that awaited the orphanage and its children. The weight of their financial struggles seemed even heavier in her weakened state.

• • •

At the bungalow man's house, Rahul was taken aback by the unexpected turn of events.

"I am sorry," I blurted out, feeling startled by the man's sudden awakening.

He reassured me with a warm smile, as if I were a welcome guest rather than an intruder in his house. "Relax, it's okay."

Surprised by his calm demeanor, I mustered the courage to ask, "Aren't you angry that I've entered your house?" Fear tinged my words.

Amused by my apprehension, he replied, "You seem to be afraid."

Caught off guard, I stumbled over my words, trying to regain composure. "Afraid? Me? Yes, I am... I mean, no, I am not." My stuttered response betrayed my mixed emotions.

"Please have a seat, Rahul," he kindly offered, pointing to a chair near the bed. I couldn't help but feel surprised that he knew my name. Obediently, I sat down, almost as if following his directive, despite his attempt to sound friendly and welcoming.

"So, what brings you here, my boy?" he inquired, his voice carrying a hint of curiosity.

I tried to maintain a façade of bravery, feigning nonchalance. "Oh, nothing much. I was just taking a stroll around the area and thought I'd stop by to say hi."

A soft chuckle escaped his lips. "Haha, is that it?" he probed, sensing that there might be more to my visit.

I shrugged, trying to appear casual. "Yeah, nothing special, just wanted to see how you were doing."

Deep down, however, I knew that there were far deeper questions I wanted to ask him, ones that had been plaguing my thoughts for days. But for now, I decided to tread lightly, maintaining the charade of casual conversation.

"It's a pleasure to meet you too, my friend," he replied warmly, extending his hand for a handshake. As I shook his hand, I couldn't help but notice the burn marks on his forearm, faintly shimmering in the dim light of the lamp.

Summoning the courage, I finally mustered the strength to ask the burning question that had been gnawing at me. "Sir, I have a question," I began, feeling a newfound respect in my voice that surprised even myself.

"Go ahead, boy," he encouraged, rising from his seat to switch on the lights. The brightness illuminated his face, revealing features that were far less intimidating than they had appeared in the darkness. Gazing at him intently, I couldn't hold back any longer. "Why do you live alone here? And why are people afraid of you?"

There was a flicker of disturbance in his eyes, and he turned away from me in silence. Overwhelmed by the impact of my words, I quickly apologized, my voice filled with genuine remorse. "Sir, I'm sorry if my question has upset you. I was simply curious to learn more about you."

I anxiously waited for his response, hoping to understand the enigma that surrounded him and to bridge the gap between the fear people felt and the man I was beginning to see before me.

"Hmmm. There's nothing wrong with being curious. You seem like a genuinely nice person. I've noticed you playing with my dog quite often. At first, I thought you were just having fun with it, but then I saw the news in the paper. It made me very happy," he replied.

I couldn't help but feel a mix of relief and curiosity. "Didn't you ever bother to stop me from playing with your dog?" I asked, unsure of what his response might be.

The man chuckled warmly before answering, "No, not at all. You and the dog seemed to have a great time together, just like my daughter used to."

Surprised by his mention of a daughter, I leaned in closer. "You have a daughter?" I inquired, my interest growing with every passing moment.

He nodded, his expression turning somber. "Yes, a long time ago," he replied, a hint of sadness evident in his voice.

My mind raced with questions. "What happened to her? Where is she now?" I asked, unable to contain my curiosity.

With a heavy sigh, he replied, "I don't know, kid. I really don't know."

"How can you not know where your daughter is, sir? I know it's none of my business, but can I help you find her?" I asked, my genuine concern and willingness to assist evident in my voice. Despite my lack of understanding of the situation, I wanted to offer my help in any way I could.

He sat down on the bed, his eyes filled with a mixture of sorrow and longing. Taking a deep breath, he began to recount his story. "Maybe it was 18 years ago when we were still a happy family. I had a beautiful daughter who was less than a year old then, and everything seemed wonderful until that one fateful day. We were on a family trip when I was suddenly attacked."

"Attacked? By whom?" I interjected, my curiosity intensifying.

He looked down, the memories weighing heavily upon him. "I was severely injured and left stranded in the middle of a road in an unknown place, with nobody to care for me."

My mind was filled with questions, and I couldn't help but ask, "Who was it that tried to kill you? Why would someone do such a thing?"

With a heavy sigh, he confessed, "It was my wife. She was the one who orchestrated the attack."

"What?" I gasped, unable to comprehend the gravity of his words.

As he continued his heartbreaking tale, the man's voice wavered with a mix of sadness and anger. "My wife," he said, his voice trembling, "had an affair with someone else, and together, they had planned to murder me. I was brutally beaten and left to die. In the process, I lost my memory. Luckily, the nearby forest tribe took care of me. It took years for me to regain my memories, and once I did, I was determined to return and find my daughter." He paused, his eyes welling up with tears. "But when I came back, there was no one here. The villagers regarded me as a murderer, claiming I had taken the lives of both my wife and daughter. They accused me of unspeakable things and feared my presence." Overwhelmed by a surge of empathy, I asked, "What about your daughter? Where do you think she might be? Could she be with your wife?" He shook his head, his face filled with a mixture of anguish and determination. "No, I don't believe so. If she could abandon me, I doubt she would have taken our daughter with her. It was always me who cherished and loved our child. I have a strong intuition that my daughter, too, has been left alone. I believe that, somehow, fate would have sent someone to care for her." His voice trailed off, choked with emotion, and I could see the pain etched across his face. The weight of his daughter's uncertain fate weighed heavily on his heart, and I couldn't help but share in his grief.

"Do you have any photos of her? What does she look like?" I inquired.

"No," he replied with a heavy heart. "When I returned to this house, it was empty. There was nothing left behind, except for the cherished memories of playing with my daughter in the small hut in the backyard." The realization struck me that the hut, where Fatso had discovered the bone, held significant meaning. Numerous questions flooded my mind, but I restrained myself, allowing the man to continue. It seemed as though he hadn't shared his story with anyone in a long time, and I was determined to listen to his pain unfold.

"I've searched for her everywhere," he continued, his voice filled with longing. "For the past year, I've visited the school, hoping to catch a glimpse of her. She would have blossomed into a beautiful girl. Maybe about your age. My precious baby, I yearned to see how she has grown."

"So, that's why you were often seen near the school?" I questioned, seeking confirmation.

"Yes," he replied with a hint of sorrow. "But the children would pelt stones at me, perceiving me as some sort of villain."

"Hmmm," I sighed, feeling a mixture of sympathy and frustration. The unjust treatment he faced from the children only added to the complexity of his plight.

"My baby didn't have a left leg, she had a mole on the side of her eye and she had a tiny extra finger adjacent to her little finger on her left hand. She would be around 17-18 years now, these are the only clues I have to find her "he said.

I sighed, overwhelmed by the weight of the revelation. The man's words about his daughter, with her distinct features, struck me deeply. She was an exact match to the girl I had known, my precious angel. Uncertain of how to proceed, my heart ached at the thought of disclosing the truth that could shatter his hopes. Despite my inner turmoil, an impulse compelled me to utter a lie, "Sir! I know her. She resides in a nearby orphanage."

My words were imbued with a fervent excitement, an attempt to revive the flickering flame of his hope. Yet, beneath my feigned enthusiasm, I grappled with the knowledge that I was fabricating a story, weaving a web of deceit to shield him from the painful reality. The weight of my own words pressed upon me, knowing the girl he longed for was no longer among us.

"There is indeed an orphanage nearby where she now resides. Her name is Shwetha," I lied, my voice faltering ever so slightly, betraying my inner conflict. Witnessing the profound joy that ignited within his eyes, I couldn't help but question the morality of my actions.

"I want to see her," he exclaimed, his excitement infectious.

"Of course, sir. Tomorrow morning, we shall visit her," I assured him, my words tinged with a mixture of regret and uncertainty. With a heavy heart, I bid him farewell, grappling with the moral dilemma I had forged upon myself.

• • •

The following morning, as I prepared to accompany the bungalow man to the orphanage, I could sense his anticipation as he waited near the gate. Clutching the cherished poem my angel had written for me, I felt its weight in my hands, a symbol of the connection we shared. But just as I was about to step out of the house, the shrill ring of the phone interrupted the moment. With my mother occupied in the kitchen, I answered the call, a familiar voice reaching my ears.

"Hello?" I greeted.

"Hello, am I speaking to Rahul?" the voice inquired from the other end.

"Yes, may I know who's calling?" I asked.

"Rahul, it's me, Anderson. There's an emergency. Please come to the institute as soon as possible," he urged, his tone urgent.

"Sir, what's the problem?" I inquired anxiously.

"I cannot divulge the details over the phone, Rahul. Time is of the essence. Don't delay, come quickly," he stressed before abruptly ending the call.

My heart raced as I absorbed his words, my mind filled with worry. I rushed to the elderly man, explaining the unforeseen circumstances that prevented me from accompanying him to the orphanage. Handing him the piece of paper with the heartfelt poem, I said, "Sir, while I may have misled you in some aspects, but one thing is as true as the earth under our feet. This poem was written by your daughter."

Providing him with the address of the orphanage, I hurriedly made my way to the defense institute, consumed by a mix of anticipation and concern.

"Choosing between the one who we love and the one who needs love. In the former we live and, in the latter, there is life." I recalled those beautiful words written by my girl on the way.

• • •

The bungalow man stood patiently in the orphanage, observing the unfolding events. Bank officials had arrived once again, determined to reclaim the land. Shwetha, with unwavering determination, fought tooth and nail to secure more time, but her efforts were met with rejection. The old man watched as she valiantly battled to protect the children under her care, realizing the depth of her love and character. In that moment, he also came to a profound realization: Shwetha was not his biological daughter.

Conflicting emotions flooded his heart as he pondered his next course of action. Should he accept Shwetha as his own daughter, finding solace in the love and connection they had forged? Or should he continue his search for his lost daughter, clinging to the hope of reuniting with his flesh and blood?

Suddenly, the memory of Rahul's words echoed in his mind, piercing through his internal struggle. "I might have lied to you about a few things, but one thing is as true as the earth under our feet. This poem was written by your daughter." He reached into his pocket and retrieved the paper Rahul had given him, the poem that had become a symbol of hope.

With trembling hands, he read the heartfelt words penned by his daughter, feeling their authenticity and love emanate from the page. Determination welled up within him as he approached the bank officials. In a voice filled with newfound resolve, he declared, "Let them stay. I shall pay the loan amount."

Confusion filled Shwetha's eyes as she questioned, "Who are you?"

Tears brimming in his eyes, he replied, "I am your father."

• • •

Anderson was deeply concerned when he received a call from the dog caretaker informing him about the missing Master. It was perplexing because Master was supposed to be securely locked inside his cage. Anderson hurriedly made his way to the cage, filled with a sense of urgency.

Upon inspection, Anderson discovered a surprising sight. Master had managed to escape from underneath the cage. Digging into the soil, he had created a space large enough for a dog to slip through and emerge free. It was a feat that none of the other dogs in the institute had even contemplated, let alone attempted. For a moment Anderson remembered what Rahul shared just before he left. "When a duck couldn't fly high with its wings, it chose to swim deep into the water with them". So, when Master could not jump over the fence, it dug a hole underneath the cage to escape and meet its original master, Rahul.

Anderson couldn't help but feel a mix of admiration and worry. Master's longing for his true caretaker, Rahul, had evidently driven him to find a way out. Perhaps, in his determination, Master hoped to track the scents of Rahul and follow them to his beloved companion.

While Anderson felt a tinge of embarrassment at the situation, believing that he hadn't been able to properly care for the dog within the premises, he was confident that once Rahul returned, he would be able to bring Master back to a sense of stability and security.

Meanwhile, Anderson swiftly instructed his security team to conduct a thorough search of the premises. Recognizing the urgency of the situation, he joined the search squad himself, determined to locate Master as soon as possible. He eagerly awaited Rahul's arrival, knowing that the reunion between Master and his true caretaker would bring the much-needed solace and understanding to the restless dog.

• • •

I rushed to meet Anderson, my heart racing with anticipation and worry. Thoughts of Master, our faithful companion, flickered through my mind. Memories of the days we had spent together flooded my thoughts, and I realized how deeply attached I had become to him. It was hard to believe that I hadn't felt any connection to Master when I first began training him, but now he meant everything to me.

I pondered over the challenge of training a police dog with a missing leg. Would it be Master's inherent abilities or my unwavering perseverance that would pave the way for his success? It didn't matter anymore.

As I approached Anderson, I couldn't help but feel a mix of anxiety and hope. What did he have to share? Was there any news about Master's whereabouts? My heart yearned for a positive outcome, for the chance to be reunited with our beloved companion. Love had transformed my perspective, and I was ready to do whatever it took to ensure Master's safety and well-being.

Love that cannot be defined, yet can be felt. It cannot be stored, yet can be shared. Which has no boundaries, yet can stay within you. It exists amidst the vibrant blooms of a garden and even within the barrenness of a desolate land. Love knows no limits, reaching across the vast expanse of the sky and the depths of the ocean. It is ever-present, visible if we open our hearts and minds to its existence.

For me, love manifested itself in the form of my Master. The pain of losing my girl haunted my dreams, casting a shadow over my existence. I believed I would never find solace until Master entered my life. With his unwavering loyalty and affection, he transformed my world. He became the vessel through which I rediscovered the sweetest memories and the joys of companionship. Being with my Master fulfilled a deep longing within me, a desire to experience love once again.

The universe has a remarkable way of imparting lessons to us, repeating them until we grasp their significance. It finds avenues to teach us through the people we encounter, be it friends, parents, or even our enemies. The lessons may come from any life form around us. The universe tirelessly churns out whatever is necessary for our growth and understanding, until we align ourselves with its teachings.

However, I have also come to realize that once we have assimilated the lessons we needed to learn, the universe has a way of reclaiming the things it had bestowed upon us. Perhaps, in the case of Master, his purpose was to fill a void deep within me, to provide companionship and teach me invaluable lessons. Once his role was fulfilled, he had to depart, leaving behind the imprint of his presence and the wisdom gained through our connection.

As I hurried down the road leading to the institute, I noticed a gathering of people ahead. I approached the crowd, straining to hear their murmurs. Then, among their voices, a chilling remark reached my ears: "Isn't that the same dog from the news a few days ago? Some reckless driver ran over it. Such a tragedy. I believe it was called "Master." My heart skipped a beat, and a wave of icy dread washed over me. I felt as though the ground beneath me was giving way.

Numbness gripped my body, making it difficult to take another step further. It was as if the weight of the world had come crashing down upon me. In that moment, Anderson's strong presence materialized beside me. He placed his hands on my trembling shoulders, his eyes filled with sorrow. "I am sorry Rahul!", his voice heavy with regret. Tears welled up in my eyes, streaming down my face, as the reality of the devastating news sunk in.

I couldn't bear the thought of facing the truth, the unimaginable loss that had befallen my beloved Master. Overwhelmed with grief and unable to find solace in that place, I turned abruptly without even attempting to see Master for one last time and ran away from my Master because I didn't want to remember the way he died. I shall remember the way he lived.

• • •

THE END

• • •